THE FALCON'S QUEST

The Falcon's Quest

John Smirthwaite

**Hodder
Children's
Books**

a division of Hodder Headline plc

To my grandchildren – Helen, Claire, Matthew, Francesca, Thomas, Jake and Rebecca

With thanks to Liu Hong Cannon and Ji Chen

Copyright © 1997 John Smirthwaite

First published in Great Britain in 1997
by Hodder Children's Books

A Catalogue record for this book is
available from the British Library.

ISBN 0 340 69820 9

Typeset by Hewer Text Composition Services, Edinburgh
Printed and bound in Great Britain by
Clays Ltd, St Ives plc

Hodder Children's Books
a division of Hodder Headline plc
338 Euston Road
London NW1 3BH

1

'All boys', said the notice. 'All village and farm boys to report to the Lord of Changdu to serve the Emperor.'

Ping He leaned on his crutch and stared at the notice pinned to the tree. The Emperor wanted *him*.

'Whue, Whue,' he shouted at the startled goats, and drove them up the path ahead of him, towards the hill farms where he lived. Breathless from the hard climb, he herded the goats into their pen, locked them in and hobbled home to tell his mother.

These were troubled times in China. The merciless hordes of Barbarians were attacking all along the Great Wall in the north. It was rumoured that in places they had broken through, and that some towns and villages had been captured, and all the people in them killed. The Emperor had taken many soldiers and young men from Changdu, and other cities, to build up the walls, and fight off the invaders.

The Lord of Changdu Province, knowing that the Army Commander was left with too few soldiers to defend the city, had ordered the notices to be placed.

'Mama, I have to go to Changdu tomorrow. The Lord has commanded that all village and farm boys are to report to the Great Hall in the city! We are to begin training to fight for the Emperor, in case the Barbarians attack!'

*   *   *

2

It was barely daylight when Ping He awoke the following morning. Sitting up, he neatly folded the patchwork goatskin he used as a blanket. Humming happily, he wriggled from his raffia sleeping mat, and, still seated, rolled it up. Reaching out, he took his crutch from the corner.

Pulling himself upright he glanced across the floor of the mud shack to where his mother slept. He tilted his head over at an angle to smile at her, for she was awake and lay propped up on one elbow watching him.

After washing himself, and dressed in his clean smock, Ping He leaned against the wall, and tidied the frayed ends of straw on his round pointed hat.

Today I'm going to serve the Emperor, he thought. *Today I will be equal to the other boys from the hill farms. Everyone knows it is the greatest honour in the world to serve as a soldier for the Emperor.*

'I am ready, Mama,' he called. His mother came to him with two rice cakes in a pouch, which she hung around his neck. She held him at arms length and gazed at him fondly. Already he stood slightly taller than herself.

'Goodbye, Ping He,' she said, hugging him. 'I know you will do well in Changdu.' She watched his slow awkward steps along the path, a crutch under one arm, a shorter stick in his other hand to give him balance.

The first cockerel began to crow as Ping He made his way down the hillside. Because of his crooked leg he had had to make this extra early start. He passed many mud huts just like his own, for here the hill farmers and their families lived. The Landowner, who owned not only all the farms, but the workers themselves, was a fat, ugly, mean man.

'He is a useless cripple and no good to me,' Ping He had heard him tell his mother. 'He can take the goats into the scrublands every day. If he can't climb back up the hills, or loses a goat, I will whip him.'

But Ping He welcomed his solitary life in the scrublands, for there, seated in the shade of his favourite mound of rock, he could watch the falcons all day.

'*Chaka, Chaka,*' the cry came from above. He looked upwards. A falcon, his falcon, hovered above. Cheerily, he waved his stick in answer to the greeting. If it were not for Chaka and his mate, life for Ping He would hold little joy or pleasure. At first Chaka had flown alone. Sometimes he would land on the mound of rock, and Ping He would talk to him. He was sure the bird understood every word he said. Often, Ping He would take home a rabbit or a pheasant that Chaka had caught and laid on the rock mound for him. Some said Chaka was one of the Emperor's falcons who had sought his freedom.

After leaving the foothills, Ping He had to pass through two villages, before reaching the high walled city. As he passed through the second village, large groups of boys began to overtake him. To cries of 'The useless Ping He!', the usual group from near his home jostled and nudged him, and tried to take his sticks. They had no time for the crippled boy who could not join in their games.

But at last he arrived and joined hundreds of boys already waiting in the Great Hall. Ping He stood quietly at the back and watched the soldiers usher the boys into long straight lines.

Shortly afterwards the Army Commander and the Lord of Changdu Province entered through the tall wooden doors. The Commander gazed over the rows of boys. Then, raising his hand high, he brought the chattering ranks to silence.

'We are the last stronghold against the Barbarians,' he told them. 'If Changdu falls, our Emperor in the Forbidden City will be at the mercy of the foreign invaders. Your duty will be to defend the city at all costs, until the armies from the Emperor's garrisons arrive.'

Ping He felt proud to be included in this great honour. No one would harm his Emperor, not whilst he had one ounce of breath left to defend him.

The Commander continued. 'Twice a week we

will have marching and combat. Everyone must be fit.'

The Lord, who had been seated on his special high chair, suddenly stood up, his eyes resting on the boy at the rear of the hall.

'Ping He!' he called out loudly. 'You should not be here. You are crippled. You cannot fight or march.'

Ping He bit his bottom lip so fiercely it began to bleed. He lowered his head, miserably ashamed. Now everyone would know, in years to come, that the useless Ping He had not even had the honour of fighting for the Emperor's life. He turned from the ranks of boys, his sticks sounding like claps of thunder on the wooden floor.

'Look at Ping He, off to watch his silly birds,' one of the bullies sniggered.

'Silence,' the Army Commander roared. He had noticed the disappointment on the young boy's face. He knew Ping He's father, a brave soldier, had died fighting against the Barbarians.

*   *   *

Ping He passed through the city's massive gates and the two villages on his homeward journey.

There were no boys about now. They were all listening to the Commander in Changdu. He passed the easy pathway up to his hill farm home, and hobbled over the hard sand-covered stony ground into the scrublands. He stopped by his mound of rock to rest, safe in the knowledge that no one ever came here. The scrublands rolled onward, as far as the eye could see. Beyond lay the Sun's Cradle. The stories told of only one man ever having crossed the fiery sea of sand; and he had gone mad, his brains shrivelled like a prune in his head.

To Ping He's left were the high cliffs, where Chaka lived, and behind them, the towering mountains. Far to his right, across the many miles of scrubland, was a straggly line of trees and beyond this the rice fields.

He sat down and looked towards the cliff face. A vulture was circling. Ping He caught his breath, and raised a hand to his eyes, shielding them from the sun's glare. Then he saw them, two small blurs streaking across the sky. They were falcons, the fastest and most fearless birds in the heavens. The vulture was threatening their young in the nest. One of the falcons broke away and plummeted. A small burst of feathers told Ping He the vulture had been struck. The second falcon made its stoop. It was Chaka. In moments, the lifeless vulture tumbled from the sky.

Ping He pulled himself to his feet; the great ugly bird had landed quite near. Venturing from his mound of rock, he decided to take a quick look at the scavenger from the skies, then return home. He had just reached the vulture when he heard hoof-beats. He whirled round.

A rider, dressed in the armour of the Emperor's cavalry, galloped across the rocky ground.

Ping He stood with head bowed as the fearsome warrior approached. The steel-barred visor of the black and bronzed helmet was lowered, making it impossible for him to see the warrior's face. However,

Ping He knew he was a captain, from the gold star on his steel breastplate.

Dismounting near the bird, the warrior threw it a quick glance, then, raising his visor, advanced towards Ping He.

At once, Ping He recognised Hai San, the Army Commander's son, a boy about his own age.

'Who are you, and why are you not in the Great Hall receiving instructions?'

'I am the useless Ping He,' he replied with downcast eyes. Hai San saw the twisted leg.

'So *you* are Ping He. I have heard of you,' he remarked. 'Is it true you can command the falcons to come to you?'

Before he could answer, other riders, whooping and shouting, galloped across to join their leader. Ping He envied them with their specially-made armour, swords and spears. They were sons of ministers and councillors from the city. But he was not secure even from them. One began tapping at his stick with a sword, trying to unbalance him.

'Leave the peasant boy alone,' Hai San ordered, 'and never, ever, taunt him again,' he added crossly, wheeling his horse.

His troop, suddenly feeling guilty at their behaviour, followed sheepishly behind.

After they had gone, Ping He climbed the steep, stepped hill pathway towards home. His mother saw him returning along the path, and knew something had happened. Despite his crippled leg, she had never seen her son's head dropped in such sadness.

All afternoon Ping He sat cross-legged on the floor.

'Why don't you go and watch your falcons?' his mother suggested.

He shook his head. 'I wanted to serve my Emperor,' he replied miserably.

The sun began to dip behind the hills, and still Ping He sat cross-legged on the floor. His mother grew concerned.

'Perhaps the Wise One in the temple could help.'

11

Ping He, his eyes tear-misted, looked up sharply. 'Do you think he would?' he asked as he pulled himself upright.

As he raised himself his mother placed a hand on his shoulder. 'It is too late now for you to make the journey,' she advised, but he had already picked up his pointed straw hat and sticks.

'I must go now, Mama,' he said, moving to the door, 'or I may never serve the Emperor.'

'Do not be too disappointed, my son,' she said, hugging him to her. 'If the Wise One does not want to see you, he will not let you find his temple!'

Kissing her on the cheek, Ping He opened the door. 'I must try, Mama. I must try.'

2

It was said that the Wise One's temple stood on the highest hill to the other side of Changdu. Ping He swung his crutch and stick purposefully across the plains. Above him a pair of eyes watched his progress.

'*Chaka, Chaka,*' the call came to him. Ping He raised his bowed head to the skies, and smiled again.

Darkness had fallen as he struggled up the hill. He rested his aching leg and looked towards the temple doorway, its brightly shining lantern guiding him along the pathway. For the first time he began to feel a little afraid. His mother had told him the Wise One could be very stern if you wasted his time. At the wooden steps that led to the doorway he hesitated.

'Welcome, Ping He.' The singing voice seemed to come from the tinkling lantern. He became more afraid. How did the Wise One know his name?

'The birds on the wing told me you were coming,' the voice sang, answering his unspoken question. 'Now tell me why you are here.'

Ping He gazed at the lantern with its hundred fine shreds of glass. 'I want to become a soldier, and serve my Emperor in the Forbidden City,' he blurted out.

The lantern glass began to tremble and shake, as if it would crash to the floor.

'You are not a scholar. You belong to the Landowner and cannot leave unless the Lord of Changdu, or the Emperor, orders it so.'

Ping He's shoulders sagged, he began to turn away.

'Wait, Ping He.' The voice became gentle again. Ping He stared back at the lantern. Its brilliant glow illuminated the hills all around, but there were no flickering flames within it. Its brilliance was a reflection of all the stars in the heavens. 'It has long been written,' the voice continued, 'that when a shepherd leads the Emperor, a peasant boy will be honoured.'

Ping He was puzzled.

'What does he mean, Mama?' Ping He asked when he returned home.

His mother shook her head. 'The Wise One is not like you and me,' she told him. 'He comes from the Gods, and only they know the answer.'

A few days later, sitting in the shade of his rock, Ping He heard hoof-beats approaching.

'Don't get up, Ping He,' the Commander's son called out, dismounting.

'How are your falcons?' he asked.

'They are very busy,' Ping He replied, surprised and pleased that he had someone to talk to. 'Look,' he pointed. 'That one is Chaka. He has a white breast with black bars across it.'

As if hearing its name, the falcon peeled off, and, with folded wings, dived earthwards at tremendous speed. It skimmed the ground, gave a slight dip, and turned skywards again, a rabbit firmly grasped in its talons. Ping He and Hai San watched together, as moles, rats, and even a snake were plucked from the ground. A foolish giant crow cawing its way across the sky suffered a similar fate. All ended up as food for the three young falcons in the nest.

The Commander's son turned away from the food-gathering falcons.

'We received a message from the Forbidden City yesterday. It said Changdu must not give in if the invaders come.'

'But if thousands of the enemy come, they will take Changdu. We have only a few hundred soldiers

16

and . . .' Ping He swallowed hard '. . . and us,' he stated.

'Yes, but we must hold out for seven days, to give the Emperor time to gather his troops and bring them here.'

Ping He frowned. He had been told that the Forbidden City was seven days' fast ride away. 'The Emperor may not know for many days that the enemy are attacking us. How can he arrive in that time?'

Hai San smiled. 'The palace official and the two soldiers who delivered the message also brought with them two baskets. In each basket were three pigeons. The Emperor said that, if we are attacked, we are to tie a message to their legs. The pigeons, when freed, will fly straight to the Bird Palace in the Forbidden City.'

'He is truly a great and wise Emperor,' Ping He said proudly.

The Commander's son stood up and began to look uncomfortable. He caught his horse's reins. 'When the soldiers arrived with the pigeons I was with my father and the Lord of the Province. The Lord has made an order. All birds of prey are to be cleared from the skies. Anyone found keeping one after tomorrow will be tried for treachery, and sentenced to death.'

Ping He raised himself up without the aid of his sticks, and, supported by one hand on the rock, pointed to the cliff face. 'Not mine,' he said angrily, and looked questioningly at the boy, whom he had now come to regard as a friend.

Hai San mounted his horse. 'I am sorry, Ping He, but they know about your falcons. The soldiers are being sent out to kill them tomorrow.'

'No!' Ping He shouted. 'They can't!' But horse and rider had galloped off.

That evening he told his mother of the Lord's order, and begged her to go to him. 'Hai San said the soldiers will kill Chaka tomorrow.'

She shook her head sadly, knowing how much her son loved the birds on the mountain.

18

'It would do no good,' she told him. 'Only the Emperor can forbid him to kill the birds.'

The following morning Ping He was alarmed to see soldiers already scaling the cliff face. He left the goats and hobbled as fast as he could to where the officer stood.

'Leave them, leave them,' he pleaded. The officer ignored him. Ping He raised his stick. The officer lunged forward and sent him sprawling to the ground.

'Soldier!' the officer shouted to one of his men. 'Take this boy away, he is a nuisance.'

The soldier gently lifted Ping He up, and carried him away.

Ping He picked up handfuls of sand, and threw them in the direction of the officer. The breeze blew the sand back into his face, stinging his eyes.

Way above, Chaka and his mate, their young under threat, began swooping over the intruders. Ping He, helpless, watched the volley of arrows as they were fired from the crossbows. The female falcon fell from the sky first, hit by two arrows. Chaka, seeing his mate struck down, dived to the attack. The soldiers lodged in the cliff face casually re-notched their crossbows, and sat back, waiting.

Ping He heard the familiar cry of '*Chaka! Chaka!*' before the arrows were loosened. An arrow was still in the bird as it spiralled down and down, out of sight, into the large clumps of gorse and bracken at the base of the cliffs.

The soldier placed a comforting hand on the shoulder of his sobbing prisoner. Ping He, wiping his eyes, watched the soldiers on the cliff. One of them reached out, his spear poking at the nest. Three fledglings tumbled out. Too young to fly, they fell down the side of the cliff face, on to the rocks below. The soldiers departed, their grisly task finished.

Ping He sat alone on the ground. He looked up at the falcons' torn nest, now balanced precariously on its ledge. His eyes saw a shadow. The vultures were already there. It was as if they had known what would happen to the falcons that day. He could not clamber over the cliffs to bury his beloved birds, but he could go into the gorse and bury Chaka. He would not leave him for the scavengers.

Reaching the first large gorse bush, taller than himself, he parted it with his crutch, and edged his way through it. There was nothing. Scratched and bleeding from his search amongst the vicious prickly thorns, he moved to the next clump. Parting the thicket, he spied Chaka. Struggling through the thorns, he thought he saw movement. He looked closer. Chaka was still alive! The arrow had caught the wing, cutting the bone almost in two. With blood running down his face, arms, and legs, Ping He carefully removed the arrow, and lifted Chaka up. The falcon opened his eyes and stared at the familiar face above him. Ping He winced as a talon fastened itself around his wrist in an iron grip.

Remembering the order from the Lord, Ping He knew he would have to hide Chaka. There was a small cave nearby, its entrance just large enough to crawl through. He would hide Chaka there and nurse him back to health. Then he'd take him far away and free him. No one need ever know.

Inside the cave, Ping He cut a slit down a piece of bamboo. Carefully setting the wing, he clipped the bamboo across the broken bone of the wing, gripping it rigid and firm.

I must check the goats next, he thought, *and find some straw to make Chaka comfortable.*

'No, Chaka, you stay here. I won't be long,' he said, when the falcon, dragging its wing, tried to follow him out of the cave.

Chaka stopped his struggle and flopped to the floor. Ping He breathed a sigh of relief.

Outside, he went to count his goats and search for Chaka's bed. 'Only the softest and the smoothest,' he muttered, snatching a tuft of dry grass from under the nose of a goat.

Back in the cave, he placed Chaka deep within its shadows. 'Chaka, you mustn't try to go outside.

The Lord of Changdu will have no mercy on us if we are found out.'

After making sure that the falcon was comfortable on his bed of straw, he went and sat guard outside.

When the sun began to sink, he herded the goats close to the cave. 'Don't worry, Chaka,' he called inside, 'I will come back later to see you.'

3

Ping He was grateful for his mother's trust. She had bathed his many cuts, and stitched his torn smock without comment when he had returned home after rescuing Chaka.

Now his cuts were healed – but he had another problem: the never-ending supply of food for Chaka. He set snares for rabbits, caught rats, and, with a fearful, thumping heart, searched for snakes. But the rocks he turned over with his crutch, to his relief, revealed nothing.

One evening, as he was about to leave his mud hut to feed Chaka, the drunken figure of the Landowner stumbled through the door. In one hand he held a long willow cane. His podgy fingers reached up and gripped Ping He by the ear and dragged him outside.

'I said you would be whipped if you lost a goat,' the Landowner's squeaky voice slurred. 'You took fourteen, now there are only thirteen in the pen.'

Ping He grimaced from the sharp sting of the cane as it lashed across his back. 'I haven't lost one,' he cried out. 'I brought fourteen back. I always count them.'

He thought how easy herding the goats had been when Chaka was flying. If two or three strayed too far, a nip in the backside from Chaka's sharp talons was enough to bring even the most stubborn amongst them back into the fold.

The cane lashed him again and again, causing him to cry out in pain.

His mother rushed forward to protect him from the Landowner's onslaught, but was bowled over by an out-stretched arm.

'I did bring fourteen back,' Ping He sobbed.

There was no reasoning with the drunken Landowner. 'You call me a liar,' he screeched, as he whipped the cane across Ping He's back and legs.

At last the lashing was over.

Back inside the mud hut, his mother laid him on his stomach and placed cooling mud on his back. 'You must rest there until morning,' she soothed.

But after an hour, Ping He reached across for his crutch. He must feed Chaka. A slight moan escaped him as he raised himself up.

'Mama, I have to go out,' he whispered hoarsely.

A frown of concern crossed his mother's face. With a slight shake of her head, she helped him to his feet, and gently hugged him.

'I trust your falcon is worthy of all your devotion,' she whispered, handing him a strip of goatskin.

Ping He took it from her and felt guilty. He'd

cut it from his blanket to protect his wrist from Chaka's sharp talons and had hoped she hadn't noticed. Since the soldiers had climbed the cliff face, Chaka had never been mentioned, and his mother had never questioned him about his late evenings. If he was found out for breaking the law, he reasoned his mother, at least, would be spared any blame.

'He is, he is,' Ping He choked, as she brushed her fingers through his hair.

The following morning, wincing with pain, Ping He struggled into his smock. He got to the pen, collected the goats and counted them. There *were* fourteen.

When he returned that evening, the Landowner was prowling around the pen counting the goats as they went through. Then, finding all the goats returned, he sniffed in Ping He's direction and stormed off.

Ping He had just finished his evening meal when the great gong in Changdu boomed out three times.

Some enemy scouts had been spotted by lookouts. The sounding of the gong meant that everyone had to leave their farms and villages, and go to the safety of the city.

'Come, Ping He,' his mother said, putting on her shawl, 'we must help drive the animals to the city.'

'Yes, Mama, but I won't be able to keep up with you. Let me take the shorter route down the hillside and across the scrubland. It will save me time.

Alone, but for the few goats trotting in front of him, Ping He made his way down the steep stepped hillside. There was no one in the scrubland to see him turn the goats away from Changdu and head for the cave.

Chaka, on his bed of straw, flapped his good wing as Ping He entered. Ping He glanced across to the bamboo casket he had made ready for just such an occasion and placed it by the straw.

'We make a fine pair, Chaka – you with your broken wing, and me with my useless leg! But the enemy is coming, and we both have to move.' Ping

He wasn't sure if Chaka understood everything he said, but the bird allowed himself to be lifted from the bed of straw and placed inside the bamboo casket.

Outside the cave Ping He quickly tied the casket to one of the goats. Then, waving the goats ahead, he made haste to join the rest of the farmers and peasants trekking towards the city.

When he arrived at Changdu, with its high protective walls, he found the guards already hurrying the streaming crowds through the massive city gates.

Up on the battlements, the Army Commander and the Lord of the Province were deep in conversation.

The Commander remarked, 'We cannot send off a pigeon yet. We have spotted only a few of the enemy. It could be a trick for us to bring the Emperor's army here, while they attack somewhere else.'

The Lord agreed. 'Tomorrow we will send out more scouts, to find out how strong their force really is.'

*   *   *

29

Ping He herded the goats into the square and untied the bamboo casket. He had to find a hiding place for Chaka. On the far side of town he found a disused hut without a roof. There were no houses nearby. 'Stay there and keep quiet,' he whispered. 'I will see you tomorrow.'

As dawn broke, and the soldiers on the walls rubbed sleep-dust from their eyes, the city woke in disbelief. They were surrounded by thousands and thousands of Barbarians. Dust clouds in the distance meant more were coming to join them. The great gong boomed out calling everyone to the square. The Commander and the Lord went to the high wall.

'It is time to release a pigeon,' the Lord decided. 'We will send two off.'

But the leader of the Barbarians had spies in the Forbidden City. They had sent him word of the Emperor's pigeons. As the pigeons flew out, he released three hawks. The watchers on the wall stared, first in alarm, then outrage, then fear; for within moments, both pigeons were struck lifeless from the skies.

'We must try again this afternoon,' the Lord said, turning from the battlements with a heavy heart.

That afternoon the enemy made their first attack. At the height of battle, the Lord released another pigeon. Again the hawks pounced.

'We must try again when it is dusk,' the Lord said despondently.

Repelled the first time by the defenders' swarms of arrows, the Barbarians attacked again that evening. They wanted the town for its food and shelter. They were hungry and weary after their long journey, and needed to rest before making their final march on the Forbidden City.

A fourth pigeon was sent out in the fading light. All eyes on the walls watched it, willing it to fly beyond the rice fields and out of sight. But it was not to be. The hawks were sent up again, and the despairing defenders saw another pigeon fall to the ground.

Ping He had spent most of his day searching for scraps of meat for Chaka. He'd heard the noise of the battle and had kept under cover when the arrows flew over the city. But he knew nothing of the enemy leader's hawks, or of their deadly reason for being brought to Changdu. More serious for him was the prowling dog who had discovered Chaka, and had barked unceasingly until its owner had come to investigate.

Whistling happily because of the bundle of meat he had collected, he reached the disused hut.

'Chaka, it's me,' he said softly, bending down to the casket. Suddenly, he felt two heavy hands drop on to his shoulders. He turned his head and saw two soldiers towering above him.

Ping He and his casket were carried back through the town. People lined the streets and shook their fists, shouting 'Traitor! Pigeon Killer!' at him. His mother stood amongst the crowds, and held her hand to her mouth in fear and dismay.

'This is the culprit, Commander,' said one of the

guards when they reached the wall. Dismayed surprise crossed the face of the Commander as he recognised Ping He.

'This is a very serious crime,' the Commander told him. 'There is no need for the Lord to deal with this now. It may well be that the Barbarians will decide Ping He's fate, and our own. Lock him up, but keep the bird alive as evidence,' he ordered the guards.

Ping He was thrown into a prison cell. The casket containing Chaka was tossed through the door after him. Opening the casket he released the bird with the lopsided wing.

'They've found us out,' he said, stroking his falcon's head. 'Now we are in serious trouble.'

All through the day, arrows shot from long bows would clang on the roof of Ping He's prison cell. Food was brought for him, and a small bowl of meat scraps was left for Chaka.

'That should feed him for a week,' the guard said. But it disappeared in one sitting.

His mother came in the afternoon, but she was afraid to enter the cell with the fierce-looking falcon, and spoke to Ping He through the bars of his door.

On the morning of the third day of the battle, Hai San came to see him. Hai San told him the enemy had not yet made a full-scale attack, but many soldiers had been killed. 'It is said we will soon be called to the walls.'

'In a few days the Emperor's army will come and drive them away. The pigeons would have surely told him by now?' Ping He queried.

The Commander's son shook his head and told of the hawks the Barbarians had brought with them, and how they had killed the pigeons. 'We have only two left now, and my father says there is no point in sending them out just to be killed.'

Hai San pointed to Chaka. 'That is why the Lord ordered all birds of prey to be killed,' he accused.

Ping He held his hand down to his falcon. 'Chaka hasn't killed any messenger pigeons,' he defended. 'And he wouldn't if I asked him not to. If his wing was healed, he would soon clear those hawks from the skies.'

Chaka nuzzled his beak against Ping He's finger.

'I wonder . . .' he remarked quietly, taking the length of goatskin from his pocket.

Hai San watched his friend gently remove the bamboo splint, and feel along the bone of the wing. 'It's whole!' Ping He cried triumphantly. 'It is mended.'

Chaka, feeling the pressure taken off his wing, screeched out in relief.

Hai San ran to tell his father. The Commander came to the cell with the Lord.

'If I can let Chaka fly, he will rid those hawks from the skies.'

The Lord tugged thoughtfully at his long thin beard. 'We have nothing to lose,' he remarked.

The Commander's face wore an uneasy frown. 'If

the enemy send up their hawks, the falcon's wing may not be strong enough for him to fend them off on his first flight.'

Ping He, stroking Chaka's wing, became worried. 'We will have to use the Great Hall.'

The Lord shook his head. 'That is where all the villagers and farmers sleep.'

Ping He stood up to his full height to assert his authority.

'There is nowhere else for Chaka to fly. If his wing hasn't mended, the enemy's hawks will kill him.'

The Lord tugged at his beard. The falcon was their only chance. He glanced at the Commander. 'Clear the Great Hall,' he ordered.

'I will need extra food for Chaka.' Ping He held out his arm with the goatskin around his wrist. 'And a proper glove.'

4

The people formed long lines, watching curiously as Ping He, on his crutch and stick, and with an escort of soldiers, made his way to the now-empty Great Hall. One of the soldiers carried Chaka's casket; another, a salver with a container of meat and a small leather gauntlet glove. This time no one shouted 'Traitor!' Even the taunting boys were strangely silent. The great doors clanged shut behind him.

Ping He pulled on his specially-made glove, and

opened the casket. Now the sharp talons would not hurt.

'You have to fly, Chaka, and fly strongly,' he told the bird.

'Go!' He moved his gloved hand upwards. The falcon flew, flapping its wings, but they were not strong enough. Ping He bent and picked Chaka off the ground. He tried again, and again. Eventually he sat down, exhausted. 'You *can* fly,' he scolded the bird. 'You *must* fly, for all our sakes.' He saw Chaka's breast throbbing from his pounding heart. Ping He looked around. He must help his falcon in some way. There! High in the roof, long ropes hung down. Chaka was gazing up at the ropes too. 'You know, Chaka! You know I have to take you up there,' Ping He said, stroking his falcon's head. He placed the falcon in the casket, fastened it to his back, and began the long upward climb. Slowly, hand over hand, he painfully pulled himself upwards. There were times when he thought he would never hold on. He couldn't use his twisted leg to help him, and the cuts on his back from the Landowner's cane smarted with each upward pull. But, after a long struggle, he reached the rafters and sat astride them. His crutch, like a small twig, lay on the ground far below.

Fastening on his leather glove, he opened the casket.

With the talons gripping his wrist, Ping He held back his arm for some moments, his mind clouded with doubts. *If the wing has not properly healed? If the bone has not fully set?*

'Please, Chaka, please don't crash to the ground,' he begged, and closed his eyes as he released the bird from his wrist.

Chaka beat his wings furiously in mid-air, but, despite his efforts, he was falling. Ping He held his breath, alarmed for the fighting, struggling bird. Then he gave a huge sigh of relief. Just before his falcon would have crashed to the ground, he saw the wings begin to beat steadily, and in rhythm.

Chaka skimmed the ground, then flew upwards,

settling on the rafters. After letting him rest for some minutes, Ping He called out to him.

Without hesitation, Chaka launched himself off, and flew to the gloved wrist.

'And again, Chaka!' The falcon flew round and round the Great Hall, skimming the floor and soaring upwards. Satisfied there was no more he could do, Ping He lowered himself down the rope. Taking the cover off the meat, he tossed a piece high into the air. Chaka swooped, gripped it, flew to a rafter and ravenously devoured it. Ping He had forgotten how hungry the bird must be.

It was late in the afternoon when he called the guards.

The Lord of the Province and all the people waited outside. Arrows flew over the walls. The Barbarians were attacking again. The Lord lifted his arms slightly, his gesture alone asking the question.

'He can fly!' Ping He shouted.

A great cheer rose from the crowd, for they knew their lives now depended on Ping He and his falcon. The Lord of the Province almost smiled and ordered food and drink to be brought to Ping He, for he had not eaten all day.

'When can we send the pigeons out?' the Lord asked.

'Tomorrow,' Ping He answered, between mouthfuls of hot rice. 'But first I must have them brought to the Great Hall where Chaka can see them.'

'The falcon will kill them!'

Ping He shook his head. 'He won't. Not if I ask him not to.'

The Lord held out his hands in a helpless gesture. 'It will be like giving a mouse to a cat,' he mumbled.

So the pigeons were brought in cages to Ping He. He picked them up and took them into the Great Hall. The doors clanged shut behind him.

Chaka eyed the birds hungrily. Ping He knew he

had only a short time to make Chaka understand: the birds were meant to be protected, not eaten.

By day-break, the people were again gathered in long queues, some expecting never to see the pigeons again. The Commander and the Lord paced back and forth, waiting for the crippled boy to come out. A hush fell on the crowds as, at last, the guard swung the doors open. Ping He stepped out with Chaka on his wrist. He nodded. 'We are ready,' he told the Lord of the Province.

The Lord bent down and tied the tiny messages to the pigeons, then placed them back in their cages.

'To the wall,' the Lord cried. The Commander lifted Ping He and carried him in his arms.

'Quiet, Chaka,' Ping He ordered, noting that his falcon was eyeing the Commander viciously.

From the top of the wall he stared for some moments at the many thousands of the enemy.

'Are you afraid, Ping He?' the Commander asked anxiously.

42

'No, sir,' he replied, 'I am just wondering why they are dressed in sheepskins, and rags, and have no proper uniform.'

'They are Barbarians, Ping He. They plunder the towns and villages and steal the clothes the people stand up in. Afterwards they lay waste to the land, and kill all the people.'

Lines furrowed Ping He's forehead. He thought of all the people in the city; even the Landowner who had beaten him, and the boys who had taunted him. He must try to save them. He spoke to the bird on his wrist. 'Chaka, you must let nothing harm the pigeons.' The falcon's eyes blinked at the early morning light. He was ready.

Ping He moved his wrist. 'Fly,' he commanded.

Cherishing his new-found freedom, Chaka sped upwards screeching out his name, *'Chaka, Chaka.'*

In the hills overlooking the city, the leader of the Barbarians held back one of his men from releasing the hawks.

'No!' he shouted. 'That is not a pigeon, it is a

43

falcon, the first one we have seen in this part of the country. Let him fly. It will help us – pigeons are their natural prey.'

Higher and higher Chaka soared until the watchers below could no longer see him.

'It has gone forever,' the Lord said bitterly. 'Now we are surely doomed.'

But Ping He knew Chaka could see them all below, even the smallest dormouse would be in his vision. 'You can release one of the pigeons now,' he said.

The Lord shrugged his shoulders, and motioned to the Commander to release a pigeon.

The Barbarian leader looked up, then prodded the man kneeling by the cage that held the hawks. 'Now that *is* a pigeon,' he said, as the cage door swiftly opened.

The watchers on the wall saw the hawks rise up. In a moment they would descend on the pigeon flying over the rice fields. The first hawk turned quickly and dived at its prey. The other two followed suit.

Suddenly, above them, plummeting at breathless speed, came Chaka. He had seen the pigeon fly up from the battlements, and knew it was in danger. At first he had been jealous of the pigeons, because his master had not allowed him to harm them, but in the middle of the night, it had been he whom his master had slept alongside, whilst the pigeons were locked in their cages. The pigeons were his master's friends, and he must protect them.

The first hawk never knew what hit it. Chaka, still in his dive, looped, and while still upside-down, struck at the craw of the second hawk. This hawk despatched in a flash, he descended on the last hawk who was chasing the weaving, dodging pigeon.

But Chaka was moments too late. The remaining hawk gripped the pigeon's head in its talons. Suddenly, realising its own danger, the hawk released its lifeless victim. Chaka struck him with such force and strength that the hawk soared upwards, before finally falling to the ground.

Now it was the Barbarian leader's turn to be dismayed.

'If they have messenger pigeons left, we can only hope other wild hawks will kill them on their long journey.'

Chaka circled above where the pigeon had fallen; swooping down, he grasped it gently in his talons and carried it back to the wall, dropping it at the feet of his master.

Ping He held out his wrist for Chaka. He did not scold him, but with his other hand lifted the lifeless pigeon, and stroked its head tenderly with his face.

Meanwhile, the Lord was talking to the Commander. Ping He overheard him say, 'Now the hawks are dead, we must cage the falcon also.'

He became alarmed. *The Lord doesn't realise the dangers the last pigeon could encounter from the skies*, he thought. He glanced across. The Lord and the Commander were still talking, with their backs towards him. 'You must follow the pigeon, Chaka,' he whispered, 'or we will all be killed.' He quickly bent down and opened the cage to release the last pigeon. 'Now, Chaka,' he said, flinging his arm out. The falcon soared upwards, high above the flying pigeon. Below them the Barbarians loosed off hundreds of arrows into the sky, and then scattered in all directions as the arrows whistled back down, hitting scores of them.

Hearing the birds fly, the Lord turned around angrily, but this time, his long, unhappy face broke into a smile. The birds were unhurt, and flying eastwards.

For seven more days, the soldiers and boys – Ping He amongst them – held back the surging attacks of the Barbarians. With the approach of dawn on the eighth day, the battle-weary, thirsty defenders began to lose heart.

'A cloud of dust,' the lookout shouted. No one knew if it was the Emperor's army or more Barbarians.

'Look,' Ping He cried joyously, his arm pointing upwards. The speck in the sky grew larger until everyone recognised the bird with the black bars across its white breast.

The Barbarians began to scatter, but they were trapped between the mountains and the plains of the rice fields. The Emperor's army ploughed amongst them, killing and capturing all but a few, who, with their leader, escaped beyond the mountains.

The Emperor himself headed his army, and rode into the city to a great welcome. He was surprised to learn that the city had fought for twelve days.

'Why did you not send word earlier?' he asked. Then the Commander told him of the enemy's hawks, and of Ping He and Chaka. The Emperor nodded his head thoughtfully.

'So that is why the falcon never struck down the pigeon. We watched them for a long time flying towards the Forbidden City. It must have thought this new basket of pigeons held the same pigeon, for it shepherded us all the way. Bring the boy to me,' he commanded.

But Ping He was no longer in the city. When the great gates were opened after the battle, no one had noticed him leave. The Lord's order still stood. 'All birds of prey are to be killed.'

After hours of searching, the Emperor was told that the peasant boy and his falcon could not be found.

'I think I know where he is,' Hai San told his father. And there, by his favourite mound of rock, the Emperor, the Commander and the Lord found him.

'I don't want him killed,' Ping He told them, his eyes glistening with tears.

A tall officer, a Major, slid off his horse, and lifted Ping He on to the Emperor's saddle.

'I will not forget you, Ping He,' the Emperor told him. 'One day, I will send for you to come to the Forbidden City.' He pointed to the high-flying Chaka, 'You are to bring your shepherd also.'

And then Ping He knew Chaka was safe.

*   *   *

Everyone clapped and bowed when Ping He re-entered the city of Changdu. Even the taunting boys gasped in wonder at the sight of the useless Ping He seated on the Emperor's horse.

But none was more proud than his mother, as she wiped a tear from her eye.

After the hill-people returned to their homes, Ping He's mother had many callers, who bowed, thanked her, and left gifts.

But memories grew short. None more so than that of the grasping, mean Landowner. He had everyone who lived on his land working every daylight hour. They had to be fit and strong to dig the hard rocky ground. Ping He and his mother were a burden to him. The boy was of no use in the fields, and his mother was only strong enough to bundle vegetables. *I want that hut of theirs for a family of healthy workers,* he thought. *It's too soon now, but before another year is out I will be rid of the useless Ping He and his mother.*

5

The Emperor, after defeating the Barbarians at Changdu, decided to visit two of his other provinces on his return journey. He cut short his visit to the second province after receiving news that his Lord High Chancellor, second in power only to himself, had died suddenly. His ministers at the Palace had, according to custom, immediately elected a new Lord High Chancellor.

When he'd received the communiqué, the Emperor had turned to his senior personal bodyguard, and close friend, the Major. 'What do you know of this Minister, who is now my new Lord High Chancellor?'

'I am surprised at their choice,' the Major replied, reading the message. 'His previous position was of minor importance, and to my understanding he is not the most popular of your ministers.'

'We shall see, we shall see,' the Emperor murmured.

Almost a year had passed since the Emperor had saved his country from the Barbarian threat. But, during that time, another threat had been fermenting, and China's whole livelihood was about to be undermined.

For over a thousand years, China had kept its silk process a secret. Many attempts had been made by travellers, merchants, and spies from the outside world to unlock the secrets of the tiny silkworm. All had ended in failure. The penalties for those caught were harsh, and many had paid with their lives.

There loomed one man, however, who was

determined to obtain the secrets of the silk process. The black-robed, black-bearded and black-hearted Prince Asirius, the only son of the King of the mighty Persian Empire. The Prince planned to murder his father and be proclaimed King. Then, with the enormous profits to be gained from his own silk industry, he would raise vast new armies from the Empire, and set out on his conquest of the world.

The Prince had formulated his plan well. Falconry was an obsession amongst the rulers and nobility of many lands, and the Emperor of China was the fiercest of competitors. Visiting Princes and Heads of State had, at great cost to themselves, tried to topple the Chinese Emperor's champion killer falcon. Prince Asirius, however, had taken steps to ensure that his desert falcon could not fail, and the high stakes for a contest between the Emperor's champion and his own falcon would include the secret of the silk process.

*   *   *

53

A mere six-day journey from the Forbidden City, Prince Asirius was inspecting the easternmost outposts of his father's Empire.

Impatient to finish his task, he thudded his sharp pointed spurs into his stallion's scarred and bleeding flanks. In pain and terror, the animal pounded to the summit of a high hill. A savage jerk on the reins skidded the stallion to a halt. The Prince swivelled around in the saddle. His dark menacing eyes saw beyond the plains and the forests, to the mountain range that signalled the borders of China.

Yes, father, he brooded, *over in that strange land will be a fitting place for you to die.*

'It is time for the Persian Empire to grow again,' he had confided to the two generals who now joined him on the hill top. One of them had the hooded desert falcon tethered to his wrist. Prince Asirius straightened himself in the saddle, and gazed down into the valley below. Along a curving narrow track he viewed a familiar scene – yet another endless procession of horses, oxen, camels, carts, prisoners and slaves, all burdened down with the precious silk cloth from China. Most of the silk below would end up in Persia. Persian ships would then carry the great bales of silk to Europe and the Far East. Always, there was a demand for more and more of the beautiful cloth. With the largest merchant fleet in the world, Persia was China's main trading partner.

The black-robed Prince's lips curled into a sneer.

'Soon all this will stop,' he growled menacingly. 'Our profits are a pittance compared to what we could have if we produced our own silk.' The Prince held out a gloved hand for his falcon, and raised it to head height. 'Now it is time to begin the start of a grand New Empire. Athens and Rome will be laid to waste. And you, my fair beauty,' he remarked to the ugly face behind the hood, 'you have a major part to play.'

Behind its hood, the eyes of the falcon had a glazed appearance. All that would change when Prince Asirius fed it the special drug his physician had formulated.

When the drug was administered through its food, the bird became a feathered bundle of frenzied, manic fury. The handlers never trained the drug-crazed bird without wearing full face and body armour.

On his return to his ageing father's palace, the Prince suggested the visit to China. 'It is long overdue,' he said. 'After all,' he added, 'they are our main source of wealth.'

The King was pleasantly surprised. His son's demands were usually about military matters, but the King had always stubbornly refused his son's pleas to raise armies for new conquests. 'Our Empire is large enough, and, as the world's greatest trading nation, we are growing ever richer,' was his sound reasoning. He was, therefore, keen to comply with his son's request. 'I will send an envoy to the Emperor immediately, to arrange the visit,' he stated.

'There is no need, Father. I will go personally, and stay there until your arrival.' Prince Asirius had already worked out his plan. He needed to spend time alone at the Emperor's Palace. There, he should find at least one senior dissatisfied minister whom he could recruit to assist him.

In the scrublands, the lengthened shadows signalled the day's end and Ping He began to herd his goats home. The troublesome goat with the piece missing from its ear had, not for the first time, clambered high up the rocks. Ping He called to Chaka, and pointed. One nip from the sharp talons, and the adventurer raced down to join the safety of the others. Approaching the foothills, Ping He noticed one of the young kids was limping. From the join of its cloven hoof, he removed a small sliver of stone. Then he began the tortuous climb up the hillside. When the goats above him had clambered over the top of the last steep rise, Ping He leaned heavily on his crutch once more, and swung himself forward.

Once on level ground he waved to the high-flying Chaka. He made sure the goats were safely locked in their pen, then turned on his crutch. But, as his stick struck the ground, he stumbled. He examined the stick. It was not broken or worn. It had become too short. Standing upright, supported by the crutch under his arm, he found his body dipped to one side. His crutch was becoming too short also. Tomorrow, he resolved, he would have to find some wood, and make a new set of sticks.

Just then, a shadow fell across his path. He looked up to find the fat Landowner glowering down at him.

The Landowner raised the stick he carried. 'I have counted fourteen goats only. You took out fifteen!'

'I've brought back fifteen, I count . . .' The heavy stick struck him across the shoulders.

'Don't you lie to me, boy!' the high-pitched voice screamed.

Again and again the stick found its mark. 'I told you you'd have a whipping if you lost a goat,' the Landowner panted at the beaten boy lying at his feet.

Ping He gathered up his crutch and stick, and painfully made his way towards his hut.

The Landowner, smirking, watched him go. Word would soon get around that he had thrashed the peasant boy for incompetence. Two or three more weeks and the mud hut would be empty.

Ping He did not tell his mother of the beating, but she saw the bruising to his face and arms.

She reached down into the hearth, then placed a bowl of hot pheasant soup in front of him, a pheasant Chaka had brought to Ping He earlier.

'You must eat it all,' she said sternly. He nodded gratefully.

'Mama,' he said, picking up his spoon and pointing it towards his crutch. 'My sticks are too short.'

His mother nodded her head. Her son was growing fast.

The next morning, stiff and in pain from the Landowner's beating, Ping He went to the goat pen. He counted the goats. *There were fourteen.* He counted them again, still fourteen. He knew which one was missing. One of the small kids. It was the one that had been limping. In the pen, he'd lifted its hoof to check it was clear before he had locked it in. He shook his head, puzzled.

The Landowner entertained guests that evening. The main dish on the menu was young goat meat.

Prince Asirius, who was within two days' journey of the Forbidden City, despatched one of his two generals to the Palace to announce his impending arrival.

At the Palace, the new Lord High Chancellor grimaced with irritation. About to put his signature to a carefully-worded document, the sound of laughter had floated through his open office window. He rose and strode across to the window. Below, in the Royal Stables, the Emperor and the Major were mounting their horses. The Chancellor smiled a fixed smile. But there were no laughter lines around his cold, expressionless eyes. *Before too many summers, I will rule China*, was his deep-hidden thought. The Major was a threat to his ambitions and he was determined to be rid of him.

A knock on the door interrupted his reverie, and he looked up.

'Enter,' he snapped, his face stern.

A junior minister came into the room, bowing low.

'An officer from the King of Persia has arrived,' he announced, handing a package across.

The Chancellor took the package and glanced at its Royal Seal. 'I will see this officer personally,' he said. As he crossed the room, he paused, picked up his quill and signed the document on the table. 'You are to deliver this at once to the Commander of the Palace Guard,' he ordered.

Later that afternoon, the Major, returning from his day of falconry with the Emperor, saw a grave-faced Commander of the Palace Guard, and a young

Captain standing outside his room at the Palace. Both men saluted him, and followed him into the room, where they showed him the Chancellor's latest decree.

Shortly afterwards, the Emperor, bathed and dressed in his official robes, sent for the Chancellor, for the customary day's reports. The Chancellor told him of the Prince of Persia's forthcoming visit, and passed across the package of letters from the King. He also passed over the decrees and orders he had issued.

Dismissing the Chancellor, the Emperor read the King of Persia's letters. A smile crossed his face. 'Ask the Major to join me,' he instructed.

There were four ministers in the room. Each one cast a furtive glance at the other.

'Well?' the Emperor demanded, puzzled not to have been obeyed instantly.

'We are unable to send for the Major,' one of the ministers responded, bowing deeply.

'He is no longer at the Palace, your Majesty,'

another ventured, and told of the Chancellor's new order.

The Emperor rummaged through his papers, and found the order.

His closest and most trusted friend was now an ordinary soldier, at the barracks, beyond the Palace wall.

The Chancellor was summoned before the Emperor. 'I conducted a security check of your personal body-guards,' he explained, 'and I discovered four of your guards in ill health, and unable to carry out their full duties. Another two found it difficult to wield their heavy swords. All were over fifty years of age.' The Chancellor had rehearsed his response to this question, days before he had issued the order. 'Your safety in the Heavenly Palace is my responsibility. I would fail in my duty to you, and all of China, if your guards were allowed to become too old to protect you. There can be no exceptions.'

The Emperor waved his Lord High Chancellor away dismissively. Wearily his head dropped. He could not react against the order. If he abolished the ruling, the Lord High Chancellor would resign, and if the Lord High Chancellor resigned, all of his ministers would be compelled to resign also.

The next day the Emperor again sent for his Chancellor. 'The King of Persia has sent me a gift of two of his finest Arab stallions. They will be delivered tomorrow by Prince Asirius.'

The Chancellor nodded, aware of the contents of the package Prince Asirius's General had delivered. He sighed, relieved that the Emperor was not in a towering rage, demanding the reinstatement of the Major.

'My stables are in need of a strong trainer, who can handle not only the horses, but the stable workers also.'

The Chancellor bowed. 'I will have it dealt with immediately,' he answered.

'There is no need,' the Emperor waved his arms slightly, 'I have already chosen a new Stable Master.'

The fixed smile on the Chancellor's face barely hid his exploding rage and fury as the Emperor told him: 'The Major is to be my new Stable Master.'

The following morning the High Chancellor was again disturbed by the sounds of gaiety from the stables below his office window. He glanced down, and saw the tall Major bend, cup his hands for the Emperor's foot, and effortlessly swing his heavily-built ruler on to his horse. Mounting his own horse, the Major took the lead rein of the Emperor's spare horse and accompanied him out of the stable yard for another day's falconry.

Later that day the Chancellor moved his offices to the other side of the Palace.

6

As he locked his remaining fourteen goats in their pen at the end of a long day, Ping He gave a sigh of relief. Once more he had avoided an encounter with the fat Landowner. They had not crossed paths since the beating, four weeks earlier. But now, as he turned to leave, he found the object of his thoughts blocking his path.

'You are not to take the goats tomorrow. You are useless, and no longer belong to me. Tomorrow you are to take your belongings, and wait at the foothills for your new owner.'

Ping He stared at the Landowner, speechless.

'Go, boy, make off with you,' the Landowner screeched, waving his podgy arms and stick threateningly.

Ping He turned and fled, as fast as his good leg and two sticks could carry him. Entering his hut, he told his mother what the Landowner had said.

'It is true,' his mother told him, tearfully. 'I have to work in the new rice fields, many miles to the far side of Changdu. We won't have a home of our own any more. I have to sleep in a long hut with other workers. The new Landowner knows you cannot work in the fields,' she said between sobs. 'He said you are to work in his carpet factory, a long way away from the rice fields, and you are to live with the workers there.'

Ping He reached for his mother's hand and held it tightly.

'Shush,' he consoled her. 'I won't let them separate us. Tomorrow, when darkness falls, I will come for you, then we will leave this place, and go far away to a new town.'

His mother gazed at him fondly, and shook her head. 'We couldn't. We will belong to the new Landowner.' Ping He placed his arm around his mother's trembling shoulders, and hugged her.

'Don't worry, Mama. After tomorrow night, we will belong only to ourselves.'

The next morning, while Ping He and his mother, each carrying a small bundle, made their way down the hillside, the Lord of Changdu Province stood in his mansion courtyard. By his side was Hai San's father, the Commander of Changdu garrison. Fifty mounted soldiers stood guard in a neat semi-circle.

A wagon was being loaded with twelve jewelled daggers, and twelve matching scimitars and scabbards, together with twelve sets of gold-plated armour. The Emperor, at short notice, had ordered the items from the workshops of Changdu, as gifts for the King of Persia's bodyguards.

The gloomy Lord shook his head. 'The King will have left before these packages arrive.'

The Commander had his misgivings too. The journey to the Emperor's Palace was long and dangerous – over mountainous terrain, and through forests, where Barbarians and roving bandits attacked without mercy.

The last package was almost secured when a soldier rode slowly into the courtyard, his uniform and face covered with the sands of the desert. The soldier steered his mount towards the Lord and proffered a message.

After reading part of it, the Lord's face relaxed. But not for long. The soldier was now at the far side of the courtyard, examining the Lord's new, and as yet unused, travelling carriage. The Lord watched him grip the wheel axle and lift. The carriage rose up easily. The Lord was furious at the soldier's cheek.

The gold carriage had taken over a year to design and construct. The new strain of wood from Burma was lighter even than hollow bamboo. The two golden dragons running full length around the coach had cost him a fortune in gold from his own vaults. There was not another like it in the whole world.

'This message states you are to take full responsibility for the Emperor's gifts,' the Lord said sharply.

The soldier nodded.

'The wagon is loaded and your escort of fifty armed troops is ready and waiting,' the Lord snapped, and turned his back.

The tall, greying soldier called out firmly, 'I do not want the wagon, or its escort. I need the packages transferring into this,' he tapped the coach's wheel.

The Lord, eyes opened wide in disbelief at what he'd heard, shoved the message at the Commander. 'Guards,' he choked out. 'Arrest this soldier.'

The Commander caught the Lord's arm. 'He carries the Emperor's seal,' he whispered.

The Lord, squinting his eyes, peered at the soldier. 'Not him,' he scoffed. 'There are three seals of the Emperor. The Emperor's new Lord High Chancellor holds one, Fu Jíang, the Master of the Falcons, holds

70

the second, and the Major, the Emperor's bodyguard, and lifelong friend, has the third.'

'He *is* the Major,' the Commander whispered.

Again the Lord squinted. 'Why, then, is he wearing a common soldier's uniform?' he demanded.

The Commander shrugged his shoulders, 'I do not know, but the message states that the soldier is to be given every assistance. If the gifts do not arrive in time, you will have to explain the reason yourself to the Emperor.' The Commander pointed to the part of the message the Lord had not read.

At the bottom of the message, the Emperor had listed many High Officials and Special Guests from his Provinces. All were commanded to attend a celebration on the final day of the Royal Visit. On the list were four names from Changdu, himself included.

With a great sigh of anguish, the Lord returned the paper to the Commander. With stooped shoulders and without a further glance at his beautiful unused coach, the Lord walked away and up the long flight of stone steps towards his mansion.

Ping He and his mother had stood at the base of the foothills all morning, and now it was past noon.

The Landowner stood on his carriage seat and pointed at the smudge coming from Changdu. 'Your new owner,' he said, rubbing his hands in glee.

'Mama,' Ping He tugged at his mother's arm as the golden coach, and its mounted escort, led by the Commander of Changdu, came into view. 'If the new Landowner is this important and powerful, perhaps we *should* stay with him.'

'Ping He,' the Commander called out, observing the crippled peasant boy. 'You are to travel to the Forbidden City with this soldier.' He pointed to the driver of the coach.

Ping He felt a gentle push from his mother. He squeezed her hand and stepped forward. His Emperor wanted him! The prophecy of the Wise

One had come true. 'One day the Emperor will honour a peasant boy.' Then he saw the tight-lipped Landowner glowering at him from his carriage. Ping He stepped backwards, placed an arm around his mother's shoulders, and shook his head.

The Commander was shocked. No one *ever* refused an order from him. He cantered across to Ping He's mother. Then he spoke with the Landowner.

'It appears the Landowner has sold both Ping He and his mother. Ping He will not leave his mother, who now has no home,' the Commander informed the Major.

The Major dismounted from the coach, and approached the Landowner's carriage.

That is the tall Major who lifted me onto the Emperor's horse, Ping He thought. *But why is he wearing a soldier's uniform?*

Ping He saw that the Commander was also watching the Major. He saw the Commander stiffen. The Major's hand had dropped to the hilt of his sword. Then the Commander relaxed. The Landowner had stepped down from his carriage and was walking in his direction.

'I have decided to allow Ping He's mother to return to her house.' The Landowner informed the Commander.

Ping He tugged his mother's hand and saw her smile. He also saw fear in the eyes of the fat Landowner.

The Landowner, trembling from head to foot, his eyes never leaving those of the Major, opened his mouth again. 'While Ping He is away, I will see that his mother is well looked after,' he mumbled.

Ping He saw that the Major had caught him smiling. The Major dropped his hand to his sword hilt again and sternly wagged a finger at the Landowner. He pointed to the sky. 'I want all the birds up there to hear you say it.'

Chaka, as usual, had the skies to himself and was watching the proceedings down below. '*Chaka, Chaka*,' he cried out.

'While Ping He is away I will see that his mother is well looked after,' the quaking Landowner shouted, loud enough for everyone to hear.

Without looking up, Ping He circled his stick in the air.

Receiving a nod of approval from the Major, the Landowner's large pumpkin of a head dropped forward with a great gush of relief.

Ping He's mother gave her son a hug and pushed him towards the Major.

'I will take great care of him,' the Major assured her gently, whisking Ping He into the coach.

Ping He did not hear the murmurs of surprise from those left behind, as, instead of turning around over the sandy, pebbled ground, the golden carriage, with its two horses, rolled forward, towards the scrublands and the burning desert.

Gliding high in the sky on the warm air currents, Chaka wheeled and set his course above the coach.

*   *   *

Hidden behind a ridge, spying on the gathering at the foothills, was a lone horseman who had followed the coach from Changdu.

At last the spy's patience was rewarded. The golden carriage had set its route. The spy waited until the returning escort had passed him by. Then he also headed to Changdu. In a disused shed in Changdu city, four others awaited his return.

'There is only an old soldier and a crippled boy on the carriage,' the spy informed them.

'The escort? What about the soldiers?' the leader of the group demanded.

'They returned here, to the barracks.' The spy flung out an arm to emphasise his facts.

Deep lines furrowed the leader's brow as he tried to reason the coach driver's tactics. Finally he stated, 'That soldier is crazy. We move at first light tomorrow. The coach and all its treasures will be ours the day after.' All five of the robbers nodded their heads to each other and smirked. This was going to be easy.

*   *   *

Far into the desert, Ping He shivered. With the setting of the sun, and night-time falling, the once-hot breezes were now cutting, ice-cold winds.

The Major reached through the open coach window behind him, and took out two heavy topcoats, and two woollen hats.

'We are going to travel well into the night,' he stated, passing the smaller coat to Ping He. 'It is our easiest time. The moon will light our way.' He flicked at the reins to quicken the horses' pace, then leaned across and pulled the woollen hat over Ping He's face, twisting it around so that its wearer could see out of the two eye slits. He grinned when he saw that his young passenger had fastened his round pointed straw hat on top of his woollen helmet.

At that moment, strong talons landed on his shoulder, causing Ping He to turn his head slightly. He reached up, and placed Chaka inside his coat.

The sun peeping on the horizon had begun its journey as the robbers left the scrublands, and headed for the open desert. The tracks in the sands were easy to follow.

In their haste to catch their quarry, the robbers spurred their horses faster. After three hours in the broiling heat, the weakest of the mounts fell to its knees and died. The begging pleas for help from the stranded robber fell on deaf ears, as the others, slowing their mounts to walking pace, passed him by.

Two mornings later, the robber's leader awoke from a nightmare. He had dreamed he was here in the middle of the desert and that two huge sand dunes, one from either side, had broken away and begun rolling towards him. They had collided on top of him and were crushing the life out of him. Gasping for breath, and freeing his arms, he pulled and clawed at great tufts of horse hair. A horse whinnied in pain, and rose quickly to its feet. Because of the freezing night temperatures, the leader had squeezed himself between two horses. One had rolled over during the night, crushing him against the other.

Panting heavily, he rose to his feet. In the faint dawn light he studied the familiar distant wheel tracks, and their scuffed centres. Nothing had altered from the previous night, when darkness and fatigue had halted them. He began to worry. Why had they not sighted the coach?

Ping He could have told him. The Major had crossed the desert many times, on secret missions for the Emperor, and knew most of its landmarks and terrors. Already this morning they had broken camp, and put an extra two hours' journey between themselves and their pursuers.

7

The robber leader kicked his companions awake. This would be their third day in the desert and water was running short. If they didn't settle with the coach today, they would have to turn back.

Whilst the others fed and watered their horses, he scrambled up the face of a high sand dune to view the landscape. An unending sea of sand met his eyes. He dropped his gaze to follow the wheel tracks. In a small valley, not too far distant, stood two trees by the side of a large pool of water. He blinked and rubbed his eyes. 'The first signs of madness,' he muttered to himself. He had heard stories of wondrous sights to behold in the desert. But the story-tellers had been insane, their minds bleached and turned feeble by the trickery of the blazing sun.

'Look! An oasis!' shouted one of the others, who'd also climbed the dune.

At the oasis, the leader, his thirst quenched, began to examine around the water hole. He touched the still-hot embers of an overnight fire, and with his boot turned over some small white rabbit bones. *If only I'd climbed that sand dune earlier, he thought.*

From one of the trees he snatched down a discarded rabbit skin, and stared at its still-moist flecks of fresh blood. He scratched his unshaven chin. There were no rabbits in the desert, at least not here. He ordered his men to mount up.

'They are only two hours in front of us,' his gravelly voice rasped, pointing out the crisp sharp edges of the latest wheel tracks. 'We will take them this afternoon and return here for the night.'

High above, a speck hovered and wheeled. The robbers were unaware that, since their first footsteps into the desert, their every movement had been watched.

'*Eeeeek, Eeek, Eek.*'

Ping He raised his head sharply to his falcon. 'There is someone behind us.'

The Major reined the horses to a stop. He did not question Ping He's statement. For three days he'd witnessed the love and understanding between the boy and his falcon.

'I can see nothing,' he admitted, after a long scanning search. 'I wonder how far behind they are?'

'Chaka will tell us,' Ping He said, and stretched out his gloved hand to call down his falcon.

The Major waited in silence whilst his young passenger talked to the falcon. Moments later, with a slight movement of Ping He's arm, the falcon flew off.

'There!' Ping He pointed to the hovering speck.

The Major studied the distance between themselves and the hovering falcon, then checked the position of the sun. 'We cannot be caught in the open if they are unfriendly,' he said, frowning, and, changing his course, he flicked the reins, urging his horses on.

The robbers dismounted in a hollow. The stationary coach stood on stony ground amongst huge boulders and craggy rocks.

One of the gang was ordered to stay with the horses. The others scrambled up the rise, unslinging their bows.

The leader grinned at the two still forms lying in the shadow of the coach, each covered by a length of black cloth.

He pulled back his bow. The arrow, straight and true, hurtled in to one of the forms. His companions released their arrows. Six arrows thudded into their targets. The leader put down his bow, and, with sword in hand, advanced towards the coach.

Ping He, holding a crossbow with its bolt set, crouched behind a rock. By his side, lying full-length, was the Major.

'Only if they mean us harm, and something happens to me,' the Major had said earlier, when passing him the weapon.

Ping He had nodded. It would not be the first time he had faced an enemy with a crossbow.

Suddenly the Major rolled from behind the rock, and fired his crossbow. The robber leader fell lifeless to the ground. Ping He stretched out his arm and passed his loaded crossbow to the Major. The Major swapped his crossbow and dodged behind the coach as the other two robbers fired arrows at him. Ping He heard the whine, then the thud of the arrows as they hit the coach. Re-notching the Major's used weapon, he heard a scream – another of the robbers lay dead. With crossbow at the ready, Ping He raised his head above the rock. He saw the third robber fleeing back to the horses, but the Major had already circled around, and a third bolt found its mark. Without fear, the Major advanced on the remaining robber. Ping He heard an order barked out. The robber threw down his weapons, mounted up, and made off with the three riderless horses.

'Why did you let him off?' Ping He asked, when the Major returned.

The Major shrugged his shoulders. 'The horses would have died with no one to look after them.'

The last of the sun's rays were spreading across the desert sands like spokes from a wheel, when the Major pulled the horses to a stop.

'We will water the horses before travelling any farther,' he stated.

Ping He wriggled over to the large goatskin water-bag that was slung underneath the coach. He quickly pulled himself back.

'It's almost empty!' he cried out.

The Major slid under the coach and unhooked the

bag. The gash where an arrow had passed through it was painfully obvious.

The Major shook his head. 'We will have to turn back.'

Ping He pulled on his leather glove. They couldn't turn back. *I can't miss seeing the Emperor*, he thought.

As he gave the last of the water to the horses, the Major glanced sideways. He saw the falcon on Ping He's wrist tilt its head as it listened intently to every spoken word.

'Chaka will refill our water-bag,' Ping He said, untying the string from his small water flask, and looping it around his short stick. 'Now, Chaka,' he said to the close-hovering bird. Chaka swooped down and plucked the open-necked flask by its strings from the stick.

Chaka returned from the water hole with the half-filled flask, almost before the Major had finished his repairs to the water-bag. Ten further journeys were made that evening, before darkness called its halt.

All through the next day whilst they continued their journey, Chaka refilled the waterbag.

For two more days, they journeyed across the desert. On the third morning they entered the shade of a forest.

As they emerged from the forest, the Major reined the horses in. 'Look!' he pointed, his arm outstretched.

In front of them, across a tract of wasteground, stood the massive outer walls of the Forbidden City.

'Whue, Whue,' Ping He gasped, bouncing excitedly on his seat.

The Emperor, glancing out of a Palace window, saw the arrival of his trusted friend, and hurried to the stables.

'Our plan worked,' the Emperor chuckled.

The Major nodded his head. 'The timing was perfect,' he answered.

The Emperor ran his hand along the gold dragons.

'Our informers in Changdu did not exaggerate. This is a carriage fit for an Emperor, and certainly not to be wasted on the lowly Lord of a Province ... What is this?' he queried, resting his hand on a splintered piece of wood.

The Major told the Emperor of the robbers in the desert, and of Ping He and his falcon.

The Emperor opened the rear door of the carriage, and saw the neatly-bound packages.

'And those?' the Major asked.

'Lose them in one of the palace vaults. I don't need them, they have served their purpose, now I have the coach.'

The Major closed the door, his head shaking with mirth.

The Emperor gaped at the splendour of the golden carriage. 'Think how honoured the Lord of Changdu will be, when one of my ministers tells him how much I admire his carriage. He will beg me to accept it as a token of his loyalty.'

'How are your royal guests?' the Major enquired.

'The King is a sensible ruler, and a good negotiator. We have agreed on many trading issues. But his son, Prince Asirius, I do not like. Thankfully, my new Chancellor has devoted much of his time to him. They are out with their falcons even now.'

The Major raised his eyebrows.

'We may be doing my Chancellor a disservice,' the Emperor commented. 'The King and I are very pleased by the way the two of them have blended together. Now, about my other guest. The one from Changdu. The young boy that took care of you – and this,' the Emperor chuckled.

'As you instructed, I have placed him with your Master of the Falcons, Fu Jiang.'

Fu Jiang's house stood alone in a wide courtyard. Behind it ran the inner high wall, that enclosed the Heavenly Palace.

Ping He was shown into a room by Fu Jiang's housekeeper. He had never been in a house where there was furniture and carpets. In cabinets, under glass-domed cages, falcons perched with eyes that no longer blinked. *A tap from one of the god's wands to break the glass, and each perfect bird could go flying to the heavens.* He smiled at his thoughts and studied one large falcon that appeared more ferocious than the others.

'He was called the Executioner, and belonged to the Emperor's father.' Fu Jiang himself had entered the room. He was exactly as the Major had described him: tall and slightly stooped with long straight white hair, a long thin pointed beard, and a moustache. 'No one knows how old he is,' the Major had said.

Fu Jiang pointed his stick at the falcon. 'He was the Emperor's father's champion. He died unbeaten in combat.' Fu Jiang gazed fondly at yesterday's memories. 'Tomorrow I will show you Titan. He is the Emperor's own champion. Titan is the only one who could have beaten the Executioner. He has taken an eagle in flight, and killed it as if it were a common sparrow.'

Ping He nodded. The Major had told him about the Emperor's champion and that it was king of the skies.

Fu Jiang seated himself. 'So you are Ping He,' he remarked. 'When the Emperor told me he was inviting the boy with his falcon from Changdu, I asked that you stay with me, instead of there.' Fu Jiang pointed out of the window to a long low hut along the pathway. 'That is where the sons of the palace ministers sleep.'

An hour later, bathed and fed by Fu Jiang's housekeeper, Ping He followed the old man along the path through the Bird Palace. Almost at its far end, Fu Jiang stopped before two of the tallest bamboo gates Ping He had ever seen.

An attendant, bowing deeply to Fu Jiang, opened the gates.

'This, Ping He, is the falcon compound. It is nearing the end of the day, and the trainers have completed most of their work.'

Ping He found himself in a wide spotless enclosure.

Lofty cages, some taller than his own mud hut at home, stood around the edge of a large clearing.

For a while he watched the handlers and trainers. They would swing pieces of raw meat tied to a length of cord, encouraging the birds to swoop and gather.

'Those are very young birds,' Fu Jiang remarked. 'Tomorrow,' he pointed across to a cage, taller and grander than any of the others, 'you will see Titan fly. Not only is he the Emperor's champion, but the champion of all falcons.'

At that moment a hush fell over the compound. The trainers stopped their callings, and the handlers brought in their birds. A large, heavily-built, scowling youth strode into the compound. On each massive gloved fist perched a hungry hooded falcon. A frown crossed Fu Jiang's forehead.

'Whilst the Emperor was away fighting the Barbarians at Changdu, the old Lord High Chancellor died suddenly,' said Fu Jiang, repeating what the Major had told Ping He earlier.

When Ping He had asked the Major why he was wearing an ordinary soldier's uniform, he'd told him about the powerful new Lord High Chancellor.

Fu Jiang nodded in the direction of the newcomer. 'The man with the two falcons is Fei Zhuang, the new Chancellor's nephew. He is a very dangerous young man.'

8

A solitary tree stood in the falcon compound. It had no leaves and very few branches. Two archers came and positioned themselves beneath the tree. They each tied a length of fine silk thread to an arrow. At the end of the thread, a piece of raw meat was fastened. The archers nodded to Fei Zhuang.

First one falcon soared into the sky, and then the next. Fei Zhuang held one hand high. When he thought that the falcons were high enough, he dropped his hand. At his signal both bowmen loosed their arrows. One falcon swooped at an arrow, and tore the trailing meat from it. The other bird ignored the bait.

Fei Zhuang grimaced and turned his back.

Ping He looked questioningly at Fu Jiang.

'Fei Zhuang has been trying for months to train one of the Chancellor's falcons to catch an arrow in flight. He wants to impress upon everyone what a marvellous Master of the Emperor's Falcons he would make.'

'Chaka could catch those arrows easily,' Ping He confided.

'Have you trained him that well?' Fu Jiang asked, a disbelieving twinkle in his eye.

'No, I only need to ask him and he would do it,' Ping He replied.

Fu Jiang recollected the tales the Major had told him but a few hours before. 'If we wanted a rabbit for dinner, he would ask the bird. Next thing the bird drops a rabbit at our feet.'

'We will see,' said Fu Jiang, calling the two archers over. Both men returned to the tree and began tying the silk thread to their arrows.

'Chaka won't need those,' Ping He said. Fu Jiang nodded to the archers who removed the silk threads and meat.

Ping He raised an arm. In a moment Chaka's talons were closed around his master's gloved wrist.

'You know what to do, Chaka,' Ping He said finally to the bird and flicked his wrist.

Fei Zhuang looked on cynically. 'The peasant boy's bird will fly in the wrong direction,' his shrill voice sniggered.

'Now,' Ping He called, when he saw Chaka begin to circle. The arrows soared. Chaka swooped and caught the leading arrow before it reached its full height. He then skimmed along and took the other one on its downward curve.

The workers, handlers and trainers, fed up with Fei Zhuang, and his ill temper, threw their hats in the air and gave a great cheer.

Chaka swooped down. First one arrow, then the second, was dropped at Ping He's feet.

With jealousy and rage, Fei Zhuang turned angrily on his heels. He would have the common peasant boy's falcon for himself, he fumed inwardly. But he would wait. His uncle, who had promised him he would be the next Master of the Falcons, had also warned him to avoid trouble until Fu Jiang could be removed.

'I am afraid you may have made an enemy in Fei Zhuang,' Fu Jiang said. 'But do not let it concern you. The Chancellor may be high and powerful, but even he dare not intrude against me or the Emperor's falcons.'

Returning along the pathway, Fu Jiang confided, 'The Emperor asked me to see if you would make a good Master of the Falcons. My answer will be to tell him yes, when you are older.'

Ping He stopped on his crutches, 'But I want to be a soldier for the Emperor, like the Major!' he exclaimed.

Fu Jiang glanced down at the crooked leg of his young companion. 'Perhaps,' he remarked, shaking his head. 'Perhaps.'

Still weary after the long desert journey from Changdu, Ping He went to his room early. He lay on the bed, and dreamed his dreams of becoming a soldier for the Emperor. He did not hear the knock on the door, or see the surprise on Fu Jiang's face at his two important late-night visitors. One was the evil Prince Asirius, about to commit the first foul deed necessary for his plan.

Standing by the side of the Prince was the Chancellor, whose greed for power had turned to treachery. He now saw an opportunity to seize the Emperor's throne.

Fu Jiang brought out his finest wine for his guests. But whilst the Chancellor distracted Fu Jiang, Prince Asirius slipped a deadly drug into the old man's drink. 'There will be no trace of the poison,' Prince Asirius told the Chancellor on their way back to the palace.

'He will be dead by the time he is found in the morning, and they will think he died naturally. Tomorrow night I will deal with Titan, then, my friend, you can say goodbye to your precious Emperor.'

Shortly afterwards, Fu Jiang crashed to the floor. The noise woke Ping He with a start. He rushed into the room. Fu Jiang was cold and scarcely breathing. Ping He scrambled to the door. A short distance away stood the long bamboo hut. He hurried to it and flung the door open. There were many boys in the hut. Some were studying their books by the light of oil lamps, others lay asleep.

'Fu Jiang is ill,' he shouted to the startled boys. One boy ran around the courtyard to the back of the hut and informed the guard on the palace wall. The Emperor's physician hurried to the house, with two helpers, to be met by Ping He. The physician forced some liquid down the old man's throat, then nodded to the two helpers.

After they had all gone, Ping He went to his room and sat hunched on the bed. There was no sign of the three wine glasses and the bottle of wine. Prince Asirius had covered his tracks well.

Next morning, after breakfast, Ping He decided to go to the falcon compound. Fu Jiang was in the clinic in the Palace, under the care of the Emperor's physician, and as yet there was no news. Fei Zhuang slyly watched the approach of the peasant boy, and called him over.

'Titan, the Emperor's champion of all champions, is flying today,' he stated. 'All other falcons are caged when the killer falcon flies.' Fei Zhuang opened a cage door.

'It will only be for a short time,' Ping He said to the trusting bird on his wrist, and gently placed Chaka in the cage.

This was the moment Fei Zhuang had waited for. He locked the cage and called over one of the trainers.

'Escort this peasant from the falcon compound. He is not permitted to return until I order it so.'

Ping He looked at the handlers and trainers for help. But they turned their gaze away. The Chancellor had kept his promise to his nephew. Fei Zhuang ruled the Bird Palace, and he now commanded the law.

For the rest of the day, Ping He sat in Fu Jiang's house.

'As soon as they open the cage door Chaka will return,' he told himself.

The evening sun was half-set when he heard footsteps on the path. He hurried and opened the door. It was one of Fu Jiang's trainers. He told Ping He that Fei Zhuang had ordered that he leave Fu Jiang's house, and sleep in the long hut with the other boys.

'Is it time for Chaka to be set free?' Ping He asked, not caring where he slept.

The trainer glanced around. 'Fei Zhuang means to keep your falcon for himself,' he said quietly.

'No! He can't! I won't let him,' Ping He shouted. The trainer stepped backwards, and glanced around in alarm.

In the long bamboo hut, Ping He sat on the bed the trainer had picked out for him. The other boys would be in soon from their studies. The trainer had told him that Fei Zhuang had chained Chaka by his leg in a cage, and placed a hood over his head.

'Tomorrow Fei Zhuang intends to remove your falcon, and report that he has flown off,' the trainer had whispered before he'd left.

Ping He stood up from the bed, and moved angrily down the room, his crutches striking noisily on the wooden floor. Fei Zhuang's law or not, no one was going to steal Chaka from him. He found some cloth and wound it around the bottom of his crutch and stick, then lay on the bed and pulled the blanket over him.

The boys were very quiet when they entered the

hut, for it was in the grounds of the Bird Palace, and they also belonged to Fei Zhuang.

In the very early hours, Ping He lifted his head from the pillow. With every nerve tingling, he glanced at each sleeping boy. None of them stirred. Cautiously, he sat on the side of his bed and gathered up his blanket, folding it neatly, the way his mother had taught him. Noiselessly, his padded crutch and stick moved along the floor. At the door he gave one quick backward glance, then stepped out into the courtyard. He passed the cages of the silent early morning song-birds, then stopped and hid in the shadows. Footsteps! Someone else was in the falcon compound!

A figure passed by his hiding place. A strange perfume lingered after the departing figure, the same smell that had hung in Fu Jiang's house when he had found him slumped on the floor . . .

Ping He quickly found Chaka's cage, and removed the bolt. In a moment, the bolt, the chain, and hood lay at his feet.

'You knew I would come, Chaka,' he said to the falcon on his wrist. The bird spread out its wings and rubbed its smooth curved beak against Ping He's nose.

'Go, Chaka,' Ping He said, raising his arm.

At the end of the compound stood a small wicker gate. Ping He raised the latch and found himself outside the palace grounds. He hesitated. He could not desert his beloved Emperor.

'*Chaka, Chaka.*' A soft call came from close above. 'I know, Chaka, I know we cannot stay,' Ping He said huskily, and began to move towards the city streets.

9

Ping He hobbled from the Bird Palace as fast as he could. He had to put as much distance as possible between himself and the Palace before daybreak. There were few people about, and the streets of the Forbidden City were strangely quiet.

An hour later, he came to one of the market places in the vast city. He spoke to a farmer, who, after selling his goods to an early morning trader, was about to travel west, out of the city. The farmer nodded towards his cart when Ping He asked for a lift.

At midday they passed through the West Gate, and Ping He hid himself under the empty sacks, away from the prying eyes of the sentry. In the afternoon the farmer stopped his cart at a crossroads.

'I can take you no farther,' the farmer said. He pointed ahead of him. 'Changdu is that way.'

Ping He called his falcon. 'We are free now, Chaka,' he said, 'but you will have to guide us back to Changdu.'

At the Bird Palace, Fei Zhuang was devastated by the news that the peasant boy had run away. He had rushed to the falcon compound, and stared in disbelief at the bolt, chain, and hood beneath the empty cage. Then he saw the Emperor and the Chancellor in front of Titan's cage. Titan was slumped on the floor. The Bird Physician, after examining the falcon, stood up and shook his head.

'The bird was perfectly fit when I examined it two days ago,' he announced. 'What happened yesterday?' His remark was directed at Fei Zhuang.

'It spent most of its day in training, preparing for the contest,' he replied, feeling every eye boring into him. *As if I am to blame for the stupid bird falling ill,* were his thoughts.

'That must be the cause of the bird's illness,' the physician stated gravely. 'Titan must have taken a bird or an animal that was diseased. Look! It cannot hold its food.'

Everyone could see the green liquid and litter that lay on the otherwise spotless floor.

The Chancellor gloated inwardly. He knew the wager the Prince had made with the Emperor. The Prince's falcon in combat against the Emperor's champion. The stakes were the secret of the silk process, against a yearly supply of ten thousand of Persia's finest stallions. The contest was to take place on the final day of the King's visit. He, like the Emperor and Fu Jiang, had seen the desert falcon, and had thought it no match for the Emperor's falcon.

'Don't worry,' the Prince had told him, 'if Titan does fly, it will be for the last time.'

A worried Emperor, returning from the falcon compound, visited Fu Jiang's sickbed. 'We both knew the desert falcon was no match for Titan,' the Emperor said.

The old man, propped up with many pillows, weakly nodded his head.

'It did not occur to us that Titan would fall ill. Is there another falcon good enough to fight the Prince's champion?' the Emperor asked.

Fu Jiang shook his head from side to side.

'The contest is only two days away,' the Emperor commented, a frown lining his forehead.

After a long silence the Emperor saw the old man's lips move. 'Perhaps . . .' The Emperor bent close, for the old man's voice was but a croak. 'The boy from Changdu, his falcon!'

The Emperor stroked his chin, then shook his head. 'The boy's falcon is not trained to fight a killer falcon.'

Fu Jiang slowly nodded his head. 'Yes, the boy will tell him what to expect.' He closed his eyes and sank back into the pillows. The Emperor held Fu Jiang's hand and considered his words.

Then the Major's account of his journey from Changdu with the crippled boy and his falcon came back to him.

When the Emperor was told that Ping He had left the Bird Palace with his falcon, he sent immediately for the Major.

'Ping He has run away. He must be found. I find I have great need of him and his falcon.'

The Major nodded. News of the sickness of the Emperor's falcon had spread swiftly. The Major sought out Hai San, who had arrived at the barracks that morning.

Late in the afternoon, Ping He at last felt safe from pursuit, and continued to follow the falcon's flight. As the sun dipped below the horizon, a chill came with the wind. On a distant hill were two huge chestnut trees. Ping He glanced up at Chaka, who was calling to him. The falcon swooped down into one of the trees, and nestled there. Tired and hungry, Ping He at last reached the hill top. Wearily he let his crutch and stick slip to the ground. Far away to his left he could just make out a large village. To reach it would take him many hours. When he had rested he would go there to find food.

It seemed he had been asleep only a few minutes when the wind rustling in the branches woke him. He scrambled to his feet in the darkness, and leaned against one of the trees. Odd pin-pricks of light showed from the village, and he decided to begin his journey now. He was about to move off when a tinkling sound caught his ears. A lantern winked and glistened across the meadow. Curious, he hobbled down the hill, and saw the outline of a temple, and wondered why he had not observed it earlier. The lantern had no flickering flame within it. Its source of light came from all the stars in the heavens. Confused, he stopped. It was the Wise One's temple.

'You have journeyed far in great sorrow, Ping He.' The voice from within the lantern said softly.

'I have failed my Emperor. I have left the Forbidden City,' Ping He replied sadly.

'You must return at once. Your Emperor has need of you,' the lantern's tone sharpened.

'I cannot go back. They will hurt Chaka, and because I am a cripple, I now know that I can never become a soldier,' Ping He answered.

'It has long been written that one day a crippled boy will throw away his sticks. Then he will stand before his Emperor in a soldier's uniform, but . . .'

'I cannot throw my sticks away,' Ping He interrupted, angrily.

A long silence passed before the Wise One continued.

'But he will stand alone. Straight and true, and the skies above him will be still.'

Ping He thought about what the Wise One had said. If the skies above were still, would Chaka not be there?

'If Chaka is not with me, I do not want to become a soldier,' Ping He said firmly.

The lantern began to tremble. The tinkling gave way to a deafening din. Ping He held his hands to his ears.

Dark clouds scurried across the skies, blotting out all but one small star, its reflection flashing off one shred of glass only.

The Wise One spoke again, his voice barely a whisper. Ping He strained his ears to listen.

'That which is written must come to pass.'

'No!' Ping He shouted. 'No!' He could no longer see the lantern or the outline of the temple. Then all became darkness. A black cloud had slid across the small star.

10

Hai San and the Major had searched the Forbidden City until nightfall. At first light, the Major said, 'I have yet to see a falcon over the city. Ping He cannot be here.' They galloped their horses through the city gates and headed west towards Changdu. An hour later, deep in the countryside, a high-flying Chaka recognised his master's friends.

'*Chaka! Chaka!*' Both riders looked up at the bird in the sky.

'It's Ping He's falcon. He will lead us to him,' Hai

San cried triumphantly, shielding his eyes from the glaring morning sunlight.

'Or away from him, should he wish us not to find his master,' the wise Major commented.

With their horses at full gallop they followed the falcon's flight. They saw Ping He climbing the remaining hill that led into the village.

'There he is!'

Ping He whirled around in alarm when his falcon called to him. Alarm gave way to joy when he saw his two friends.

The Major told Ping He of Titan's sickness, and of the Emperor's gamble with Prince Asirius. 'We will lose the secret process of the silk, and, far worse, we may lose the Emperor. He feels he will no longer be able to rule if the silk process is lost through his mistake.'

The two riders anxiously awaited Ping He's answer. But he could not answer. He was being asked to send Chaka to fight a trained killer. Would this mean the end for Chaka? The Wise

One had told him he would stand alone before the Emperor.

Hesitantly he slipped his hand into his leather glove.

With Chaka on his wrist, he walked away from his two friends, and sat on the hillside. Finally, he raised his hand slightly, and watched his falcon soar upwards.

'It is Chaka's decision,' he said, joining the others.

The three friends watched the bird climbing higher, ever higher. Suddenly, with its loud distinctive cry of *Chaka*, *Chaka*, the falcon turned east.

'He is going back, he is going to fight for us,' Hai San shouted.

Ping He bit his lip fiercely, but felt no pain.

That night in a room at the Palace fit for a prince, he slept very little. The Wise One's prophecy repeated itself over and over in his mind. 'You will stand alone before the Emperor. You will stand alone before the Emperor.'

'Chaka, why?' Ping He murmured. 'When I had given you your freedom?'

The break of dawn heralded the last day of the King's visit. At the foot of the palace steps, the Emperor and the Major waited patiently for Ping He and Chaka.

'I want you to come back to me,' Ping He half-pleaded, and half-scolded, before Chaka flew off.

'Come, Ping He, there is work to be done this day,' the Emperor said, opening his carriage door.

After a short journey to the outside wall, the coach stopped.

A tall wooden platform, as high as the wall itself, had been built.

'When everyone else is seated, I will take you up,' the Major said quietly.

Ping He watched the Emperor, the King, Prince

Asirius, and the Lord High Chancellor climb the steps.

'Come,' the Emperor crooked a finger when he saw Ping He arrive on the platform.

'You are in Ping He's seat,' the Emperor said to his Chancellor. The treacherous Chancellor, angry at being forced to move from the Emperor's side by a peasant boy, smiled his false smile, and walked along the platform to sit by the Prince.

The platform overlooked the wasteland. On one side was the forest. On the other, reaching down from the mountains, huge craggy rocks and boulders were scattered.

Prince Asirius leaned across. 'Shall we begin the contest?' he asked.

Ping He looked up at Chaka, a tiny speck in the sky.

The Emperor pointed to the wheeling bird. 'My champion is waiting,' he responded.

'But I heard that Titan had been taken sick,' Prince Asirius queried.

'The contest is between my champion, and your desert falcon,' the Emperor replied. 'There is my champion,' the Emperor pointed upwards again.

The Prince gave the Chancellor a questioning glance.

'It is the crippled urchin's bird,' the Chancellor whispered. 'It is not a trained killer,' he added.

Prince Asirius gave an evil grin. It did not matter what bird flew in the sky. He had given his desert falcon enough drugs to down two Titans. Even now, his bird's frantic squawking and screeching could be heard halfway across the Forbidden City.

'So be it,' the Prince said, and nodded to his handlers below to free the crazed bird from its cage.

From his great height Chaka saw the bird climbing fast towards him. He also saw his master seated on the high platform. 'You will be in mortal danger from one of your own kind,' his master had told him after he'd refused to fly to other realms. But, had not his master once put his own life in mortal danger for

118

him? Although he had no personal quarrel with this falcon from a different tribe, its murderous intent was obvious. It was not only a threat to himself, but to his master also, and had to be slain.

The watchers on the ground held their breath as the falcon in the heavens dived.

Chaka decided to give this intruder into *his* skies the benefit of the doubt and at the last second veered away. His hopes that the desert falcon would recognise the gesture and leave melted. The passing killer's eyes were awash with madness and hate.

Turning, Chaka felt the cool shadow of the killer's wings above him as they blotted out the sun.

Sharply folding his wings, Chaka stopped, held still for a moment, then dropped. With a frightening scream the attacker's outstretched talons skimmed within an inch of his head.

Prince Asirius grinned at the Chancellor. 'My falcon will strike him next time.' He threw out his hands and clapped them together. 'Pouf! Then it will all be over.'

119

Ping He never felt the comforting arm the Emperor placed around his shoulder. He was willing Chaka to avoid the deadly menace in the skies.

Chaka saw the killer streaking towards him. He waited until the last moment. With wings folded tight, he rolled. His sharply outstretched talon seared the desert falcon's breast. The killer screamed out in anger. With froth streaming from its mouth, it dived on its intended victim, only to see it plummeting towards the ground.

'He has it now,' Prince Asirius shouted, jumping up from his seat.

But Chaka had other thoughts. That morning, searching for his breakfast, a raven had flown out of the forest. He'd swooped, but the raven had sighted him, jinked from his path and sped across the wasteground. This did not worry Chaka for he could quickly overtake his prey. The raven had headed for a chasm between two huge rocks in the wasteland, and flown through it into the mouth of a wide cave. Chaka had followed headlong in pursuit but the raven had disappeared. Instead, a solid wall of rock appeared to be rushing towards him. Instinctively, he'd curved to his right. His wings brushed the rock face, and then he was in the open again. He'd spared the raven and let it have its earned freedom.

With the killer falcon's beak snapping at his tail feathers Chaka held course for the two huge rocks, and sped between them. At breakneck speed they entered the cave. Chaka knew the short distance from the mouth of the cave to the wall. At the last moment he curved to his right. He heard the thud whilst still in his curve. Then he was out into the open.

The watchers on the platform waited until it became apparent that the desert falcon would never take to the skies again.

The evil Prince's eyes narrowed. His falcon had failed him. He removed his turban to mop his brow. The two longbowmen hiding at the edge of the forest noted the pre-arranged signal from their paymaster. Carefully they took aim at their targets: the Emperor and the King.

A hush came over the crowds when they heard the whine of arrows. Chaka, circling above, hurtled down. He had seen the arrows aimed and loosed. His master stood in danger. Within inches of the King and the Emperor, Chaka snatched one then the other arrow. With his loud cry of '*Chaka, Chaka*', he circled and dropped them both at Ping He's feet.

Ping He blushed crimson when the Emperor lifted him high above his head to receive the crowd's deafening cheers.

Many troops were sent to search the forest, but the Prince had planned his treachery well. The two assassins' arrows had been captured from the Barbarians, and cunningly used so no one could accuse his troops of having fired them. Instead of collecting the rich reward promised them, the assassins were slain by a group of Prince Asirius's waiting troops. Their bodies and weapons were buried in two shallow graves already prepared in the forest.

After the evening banquet, the Emperor's guests were entertained by dancers, acrobats and jesters. But as the hour grew late, no one noticed a sleepy-eyed Ping He leave the great hall through a side door. Slowly he moved along a short passage, and found himself in the Royal Stable-yard. He would go and say goodnight to the black stallion. Ping He had seen the horse earlier in the day, its flanks scarred and bleeding from the Prince's wickedly pointed spurs, and he had bathed the wounds of the frightened animal.

About to turn a corner he heard low voices. He shrank back. One of the voices belonged to the Lord High Chancellor. Ping He peered around the corner. The Chancellor was passing a small tray to Prince Asirius, the same tray in which silkworms were reared. The Prince handed it to his two generals who were underneath the King's coach. Prince Asirius then held out his hand. The Chancellor felt inside his robe, and produced a scroll. 'Guard it well,' he said.

'All the information is here?' Prince Asirius queried.

Ping He made to move. He must warn the Emperor. His balancing stick, which he had not yet replaced, lurched him over on the cobbled yard. Thrown off balance, he let go of the stick which clattered to the floor.

He never felt the blow that crashed down on his head. Prince Asirius smiled cruelly at the unconscious figure at his feet and dragged him across to where the coach stood.

'It is the common urchin boy,' the Chancellor exclaimed.

Prince Asirius withdrew his curved sword. 'He has interfered with my plans for the last time,' he snarled, raising the sword above his head.

The Chancellor gripped the sword arm.

'Not here,' he said, pulling the Prince away. 'There is a better place.'

The evil Prince laughed when the Chancellor explained his plan. He called to his two generals and beckoned them over.

11

With the sun rising steadily behind him, Chaka began circling the Palace, calling for his master.

The Emperor, walking in the gardens, looked up. 'That is the boy's falcon,' he stated.

Chaka continued calling and circling the Palace.

The Emperor became uneasy. 'Bring the boy to me,' he commanded.

Summoned before the Emperor, the High Chancellor appeared. 'The crippled boy has run off again,' he announced smugly.

'Without his falcon?' The Emperor reacted angrily, and pointed to the bird. The Chancellor's mouth dropped open. He had not taken Chaka into account when he had made his plan to get rid of Ping He.

'Search every corner of the Palace, and send troops all over the city,' the Emperor ordered. Then he sent for the Major.

Together they discussed the mysterious disappearance of Ping He. The Emperor ordered the boy to be found at whatever cost.

The Major collected Hai San. 'If we have to search all of China, Ping He must be found. But I think our best chance of success lies up there.' The Major pointed to the circling falcon.

When Ping He awoke from his blow, he found himself bumping along, face downwards, across the saddle of a horse. His head throbbed and his shoulder ached. Then he remembered. He had seen the Lord High Chancellor passing the secret of the silkworm to the foreigner, and then his stick had slid from under him. Ping He focused his eyes on the ground. He was in the desert. He turned his head, and stared into the face of the rider of the horse. Ping He recognised him as one of Prince Asirius's generals. The General glared back at him and galloped across to his companion. Next moment, Ping He felt himself tumbling through the air to land with a thud on the soft sand. The second rider threw his crutch and stick to the ground. Without a backward glance, they trotted their horses away.

'Don't leave me here,' he croaked, scrambling to his knees.

But Prince Asirius's heartless generals took no heed.

He watched the departing horsemen until they became ghostly shapes in the shimmering desert sun.

Feeling the sun beginning to burn through him, Ping He gathered up his crutch and stick, and began walking in the direction of the footprints. After a few yards he fell, exhausted. A large rock amongst some stony ground lay not far away. With his head throbbing, he crawled towards it, hoping to find shelter, but the sun climbing the heavens cast its burning heat everywhere.

Wearily, he sank down by the rock and through the haze watched a bird winging idly above.

'Chaka!' For a brief moment, relief shone in his eyes, and the glimpse of a smile crossed his face, then he recognised the chilling menace above.

'Oh no,' he croaked. Gripping his stick firmly, he huddled closer to the rock, and turned his head upwards again. 'Chaka,' he cried out, 'Chaka, help me.'

The vulture, unhurried, ever-patient, recognised the signs of helplessness and began to circle. But the blistering sun, its thirst unquenched, sucked remorselessly at its dust bowl and drew Ping He's cries upwards, into the heavens. And the winds became alive with whispers.

Chaka suddenly stopped his circling of the city, and sped with the winds.

'The bird is flying away,' Hai San cried, and spurred his horse.

The Major shot out his arm and gripped the reins of his young companion's horse. He shook his head. 'It's flying too fast, we could never keep up.'

Hai San relaxed his reins. Chaka was already out of sight.

Within minutes Chaka had cleared the forest and sped over the desert. From a long distance he saw the circling vulture. Below, by the side of a large boulder, lay the huddled figure of his master. The vulture, hovering like a kite on a long piece of string, was unaware of the approaching blur. Chaka, wings folded, speared down like a meteor, his strong head and beak ramming into the long neck. He never gave a second glance at the ugly predator as it dropped, lifeless, from the skies, but in the distance a large flock of its kind was fast approaching.

Chaka hovered above the still figure on the ground, screaming out to be heard.

Ping He felt the coolness of the fanned breeze from Chaka's wings, and faintly heard his falcon's cries.

'Chaka, I knew you would come,' he murmured weakly, and tried to raise his arm.

Chaka swooped and gathered the short balancing stick from the sands. In a short while the vultures would be circling.

Hai San and the Major scanned the skies, impatient for the falcon's return.

'There,' the Major pointed, taking note of the sun's position. 'If he has found Ping He, he is more than three hours' hard ride away,' he stated.

Close above them, Chaka released the stick.

'It is Ping He's,' Hai San said, retrieving it, and handing it to the Major.

'*Chaka, Chaka,*' the falcon screeched.

'Quickly!' the Major shouted, and he reined his horse in the direction of the flying bird.

Other soldiers began to mount their horses also, but the Major and Hai San were already through the

131

gates. Swiftly they raced through the forest. Clear of the stinging, whipping branches, they thundered across miles of rocky scrubland into the desert. The Major slowed his horse to a gentle trot, and pointed to the shimmering heat.

'We dare not lose our horses,' he told a frowning Hai San.

Now deep into the desert, Chaka, with his long-range vision, could see the flock of vultures wheeling above his motionless master. Others were straggling in to join them for the expected feast. He flew down again and again, calling to the riders, urging more haste.

The Major reached for his goatskin water bottle, and untied its neck. Hai San watched him loop a thong loosely over Ping He's stick, and carefully hold out the bottle. His head ducked sharply as fluttering wings brushed his hair. The bottle was whisked away, gripped firmly in Chaka's talons.

'Ping He taught me that on our journey from Changdu,' the Major explained to a surprised Hai

San. 'Look, the bird knows we no longer need him.'
The Major's eyes were fastened on the two sets of
hoofprints in the soft sand.

Ping He lay on his side by the rock. Seated within
yards of him, like grotesque stone gargoyles from a
church rampart, were three vultures, their soulless
eyes watching and waiting.

Chaka flew down, and placed the bottle at Ping
He's hand. He cried out loudly. But there was no
response. Carefully he tilted the bottle, pouring
the contents over the still face. He tugged at Ping
He's smock, trying in vain to pull the exposed face
closer to the rock. Above, the foul black shapes were
circling ever lower. With a loud, fearsome shriek, he
launched himself into the skies.

'Look.' The Major urged his horse to a gallop.
Hai San saw two vultures circling in the distance.

'We may be too late,' the Major shouted. 'They

gather in flocks when a victim is sighted.' Then the Major saw the huddled form near the rock. He raced across – there was a bird at Ping He's face. Groups of vultures feeding off their own kind flapped their wings irritably at the intrusion. The Major jumped from his horse. The bird lying across Ping He was Chaka. A broken wing lay across the boy's face, shielding it from the boiling sun. The Major gently moved the motionless falcon away. He cradled Ping He's head, and began to force water between the cracked and swollen lips. He noted the wound on the boy's head, and the bruising of his shoulder. The Major looked at Hai San who was bathing blood from the falcon's head. Hai San caught the Major's gaze. His eyes brimmed with tears as he held out the blood-soaked broken body of the falcon.

'I think Chaka is dead,' he said.

The Major went to his horse, and returned with a blanket.

He secured one end on the rock, and with

Ping He's crutch supported the other end off the ground.

'It will afford you both shelter until the troop arrives.'

Hai San felt a dreadful fear at the steely tone, and the intense cold stare in the Major's eyes. Without another word the Major collected his horse, and, walking slowly in front of it, began to follow the tracks in the sand.

It was dark when the returning troops entered the city gates.

Fu Jiang, now well recovered, stood at the Emperor's side as Ping He and his falcon were brought into the palace.

'He could not have survived much longer,' the physician told the Emperor after Ping He was placed in the clinic.

Fu Jiang, standing near the table on which Chaka lay, shook his head slowly, in response to the Emperor's querying glance.

'It must have put up a dreadfully grim struggle,' the captain of the troop said. 'We counted eleven slain vultures around the boy.'

'When the Major returns we will discover the truth,' the Emperor said quietly.

In the gathering gloom the Major followed the line of prints in the sand. He knew exactly where the two killers would be resting, some three hours farther away. Pursuit would be the furthest thought from their minds.

It was dawn when the Major re-entered the city. A troop of soldiers escorted him to the Palace.

The Emperor sat grim-faced on his throne as the Major told him of how Fu Jiang had nearly died, of the treachery of the Lord High Chancellor, the poisoning of Titan, and the attempts on the King's and the Emperor's lives.

'Prince Asirius still plans to kill the King,' the Major continued. 'He has a troop of his own men dressed as Barbarians. Three days' journey from here they intend to ambush the King's party and slaughter them all. Prince Asirius also has a tray of silkworms hidden under the King's coach, and a copy of the scroll,' the Major ended.

The Emperor had no need to ask the Major how he had gained his information, nor of the fate of the two generals. He beckoned to the Commander of Changdu, and gave him whispered orders. Then he summoned the Commander of the Palace Guards.

A few minutes later, the Lord High Chancellor stood in chains before the Royal Throne. Gone were his ambitions to rule China.

The Commander of the Palace Guards passed an ornately carved casket to the Emperor. 'We discovered it while searching his rooms,' the Commander stated.

The Emperor glanced at the casket. It was a replica of the one his ministers used to register their secret votes. His Chancellor had used it to get himself elected.

'Throw him in the dungeons,' the Emperor said in disgust. 'In due time I will consider his fate . . . And put his nephew, Fei Zhuang, in with him for company.'

The Emperor clapped his hands dismissively, then raised a hand slightly, signalling the Major to stay.

'I have sent the Commander of Changdu with a thousand troops to encircle the ambush area,' he told the Major. 'He has instructions to make sure the King is not harmed, but that the Prince perishes, along with his assassins.'

'How is the boy?' the Major asked.

'He will recover,' the Emperor replied.

'And his falcon?'

The Emperor shrugged his shoulders. 'I am afraid the falcon is dead.' He saw the dismay on his friend's face. 'Thankfully, the boy will at least be spared the sight of his torn and broken falcon.'

'You've buried it so soon?' the Major asked, mildly surprised.

The Emperor shook his head. 'There was a great

storm in the early hours, and the river burst its banks. The separate cage in which Ping He's falcon was placed was swept away. It was probably kindest,' the Emperor tailed off softly.

After three days of care, Ping He briefly opened his eyes.

'Where is Chaka?' were his first croaked and mumbled words.

'We cannot allow a falcon in the Heavenly Palace,' soothed Fu Jiang.

Reassured, and with what passed as a smile at the answer, Ping He re-closed his eyes.

The physician and the Emperor were also at the bedside. The physician took the Emperor to one side.

'The boy's knee is twisted in its socket. I believe it can be corrected if we are allowed to operate. The acupuncture will ensure he feels no pain.'

The Emperor returned to the bedside, and stared at the sleeping boy.

'When he is well enough, do it,' he commanded.

The following day, Ping He asked to see Fu Jiang.

Seated by his bedside, Fu Jiang explained. 'He died trying to save you.'

Ping He, his face flooded with tears, turned and buried his head in the pillows.

The old man stood, patted the heaving shoulders, and, wiping away his own mist of tears, walked to the door.

12

As the weeks passed, Ping He remained hunched on his bed, except for one hour each day.

The physician spoke to the Emperor, and told him of his concern for his young patient.

'The operation to his leg was successful, but the boy is very pale and rarely speaks. Each day he traces the same walk, following the path of the floods that swept his falcon away.'

The Emperor stroked his chin, a thoughtful expression on his face. He sent for the Major.

One morning when Ping He opened his eyes, he saw his mother gazing into his face.

He lay his head on her shoulder and wept. 'Mama, I have lost Chaka,' he cried in anguish.

'I know,' she said, saddened at her son's sorrow.

'Look, Mama!' For a moment Ping He put his aching heart aside, and wriggled from his mother's comforting hug.

His mother clasped her hands together and marvelled as her son, taller now, strode across the room without his sticks. But then she became concerned at how thin he appeared. 'Perhaps if you saw the Wise One he could help you again,' she suggested.

Ping He shook his head. 'The Wise One is very angry with me,' he whispered.

'The Wise One is full of wisdom, he will listen,' she told him.

Ping He looked past his mother's shoulder. In the doorway stood Hai San and the Major.

'The Emperor commanded me to return,' Hai San said, struggling free from Ping He's hug.

A few days afterwards, the Major sought out Ping He and, taking him to a room next to his own at the barracks, the Major handed him a uniform.

'The Emperor is to review his troops tomorrow,' he told Ping He. 'We are to be present at his parade.'

Ping He held the uniform, and felt the smooth richness of its fine silk. He was to become a soldier.

The next day, all of the Emperor's guards stood in long columns. Their gold breastplates, helmets, spears and shields glinted in the morning sunlight.

The Emperor appeared, and climbed the platform to salute his parading guards. After the soldiers had marched past, the Emperor, escorted by three generals, came down from the platform.

First the Emperor spoke to the Major, who still wore his ordinary soldier's uniform. The Emperor pinned a ribbon to his chest and Ping He saw that the Major could once again wear his proper uniform.

Next the Emperor pinned a similar ribbon to Hai San.

The Emperor moved in front of Ping He. 'For you, who will one day be my finest General,' he told him, as he pinned a Major's medal on to his tunic.

From behind the platform an officer appeared, leading the black stallion that had belonged to Prince Asirius. The officer handed the reins to Ping He. The Emperor, smiling, returned to the platform.

The black stallion nuzzled Ping He. The scars on its flanks were healed, and gone was the lurking fear from his eyes.

Ping He looked down to the ribbon on his uniform, and then over to the platform where his mother sat at the Emperor's side. This time he could not stop the tears of pride that blurred his vision. Then a great sadness came over him. The words of the Wise One echoed through him.

'He will stand alone, straight and true, and the skies above him will be still.'

Ping He glanced upwards. There were no welcoming cries, the skies were still and empty.

The Major noticed the pained suffering on Ping He's face, and walked with him to the stables.

'I understand the great ache in your heart,' the Major said. 'Perhaps we should go away from this place of sad memories for a few days,' he suggested.

Ping He thought of the words of his mother. 'The Wise One is full of wisdom, he will listen.'

He mounted the black stallion and gently released the firm hand with which the Major had gripped him.

'This is a journey I must make alone,' he said.

Ping He rode through the Forbidden City, and followed the same route he had taken in the farmer's cart those many weeks ago. This time there was no hiding under sacks, and the guard at the gate saluted him when he rode past.

At the two chestnut trees, now heavily laden with their fruits, Ping He dismounted, and left the stallion to graze in the lush meadow. He stared across at the wood. There was no sign of the temple, and he wondered if he had found the correct place. His stallion whinnied and nervously pawed at the ground. He turned to the fretting animal, then spun back sharply at the tinkling sound that came from the woods. The temple! Ping He stared. On its highest pinnacle, with his back towards him, perched his falcon.

'Chaka,' he mouthed softly. 'Chaka! Chaka!' he shouted joyously, running down the hill.

'We were expecting you, Ping He,' the Wise One's voice boomed.

'I came to ask for your help, for I had lost Chaka.'

'Then you may go away contented, for you have found him.'

'Chaka,' Ping He called out. Chaka, still with his back towards him, ruffled his feathers, and ignored the call.

'Why does he not come?' Ping He asked.

'He is not yours to command,' the Wise One answered.

'He belongs to me,' Ping He cried out.

'The falcon has never belonged to you.'

'I do not understand,' Ping He said.

The lantern tinkled in the breeze. 'At the moment of your birth Mother Earth made a mistake. Mountains moved, and the earth shook. The house you were in crashed down. Mother Earth saw you brought from the rubble. She was saddened by the injuries to the newborn infant, and she came to me for help. I promised to watch over you.'

'What has that got to do with Chaka?' Ping He questioned.

'I journeyed far and long to a world which you do not know, and I sought out the Oracle, where the Immortals and the Gods go for guidance. When I returned, the falcon was on my pinnacle. The Oracle had sent it to assist me, it became my eyes in your world. Now the falcon's quest is completed.'

'He is mine! Chaka and I belong to each other,' Ping He answered back.

The lantern's shreds of glass jangled noisily. 'The Oracle is jealous of all his possessions. The falcon belongs to the Oracle, and must be returned.'

Ping He glanced up at the pinnacle, but Chaka, and the temple, had vanished.

'Don't you understand!' he shouted at the slumbering trees. 'I cannot leave without Chaka! He would never desert me.'

But there was no response. Even the breeze had gone.

Ping He returned up the hill to the two chestnut trees, and sat motionless, staring at the wood below.

Night came, then the dawn, and then again the night and the dawn. Ping He felt weak, for no drink or food had passed his lips. The sun began to sink again, casting long shadows from the surrounding hills. He had given up hope of ever leaving the meadow, when a familiar tinkling sound caught his ears.

Unsteadily, he stumbled towards the wood, to the glinting lantern. He reached for a branch from a tree and pulled himself upright.

'Ping He,' the Wise One said quietly. 'I cannot give you the falcon. If you do not leave here you will die, and the falcon will die also, for he has taken neither food nor drink for three days.'

Ping He sighed deeply. The Wise One was right. He would lose everyone, all of his friends, his Emperor, even Chaka, if he stayed. He would have to make one last plea now or Chaka would be lost forever.

'If I ask the Emperor to order his physician to return me to my crutch and stick, and send me back to the goats at Changdu, will you release Chaka for me again?' he pleaded.

The last rays of sun were glinting on a few lantern

shreds only. Ping He prayed that the temple would not disappear.

'Even I cannot face the wrath of the Oracle,' the Wise One boomed back angrily. 'No one has more power than the Temple of the Gods.'

A sudden stillness fell over the meadow. The ground around Ping He began to tremble. Anxiously he wiped his hand across his grime-laden face and eyes. The woods in front of him began to dip and sway like a small boat on the ocean surface. The sound of a thousand drums was beating behind him.

He spun around. The fruits of the two large chestnut trees were hammering to the ground like giant brown hailstones. Then all became still.

'Ping He,' the Wise One's voice boomed out. 'It appears even the mightiness of the Oracle bows before your friend Mother Earth.'

Ping He barely heard the Wise One's words. From long habit, his arm began to rise up from his side.

His senses had caught the sound of fluttering wings. A pair of talons gripped his wrist.

'Chaka!' Ping He screamed out. Furtively he hid the falcon in his tunic, and faced the temple, but it had gone.

With tears streaming down his face, he kissed the feathered head, and saw the terrible scars. Then two huge billowing clouds began forming above the woods.

Ping He dashed up the hill to his stallion, who was tossing his head uneasily and pawing at the fallen fruits. He glanced towards the wood, the two clouds were drifting towards him. Quickly mounting the stallion, he pressed his heels into its flanks and released Chaka from his tunic.

A fearful crash of thunder burst from the first cloud, its frightening din booming and crashing around the hills.

From the following cloud, showers of warm refreshing water tumbled, to moisten parched lips.

'Chaka, Chaka.'

Ping He slowed his mount and looked up. The clouds had become mere wisps of fast-disappearing smoke.

Ping He smiled, pulled on his glove, and called to the hovering falcon.

'The Wise One said that the falcon's quest was complete, Chaka,' he told the bird on his wrist. 'But for us it is just the beginning . . .'